DAY AND DASTAN

Two novellas

INTIZAR HUSAIN

TRANSLATED BY
Nishat Zaidi and Alok Bhalla

NIYOGI
BOOKS

Published by
NIYOGI BOOKS
Block D, Building No. 77,
Okhla Industrial Area, Phase-I,
New Delhi-110 020, INDIA
Tel: 91-11-26816301, 26818960
Email: niyogibooks@gmail.com
Website: www.niyogibooksindia.com

© Nishat Zaidi and Alok Bhalla

Cover design: Misha Oberoi
Layout: Shashi Bhushan Prasad

ISBN: 978-93-86906-27-4
Publication: 2018

Printed at: Niyogi Offset Pvt. Ltd., New Delhi, India

Introduction

by Nishat Zaidi

The fictional world of Intizar Hussain [1925–2016], one of the greatest Urdu writers, and most certainly a world writer, is as enmeshed in the cataclysmic events of the 1947 Partition of the Indian subcontinent, as was his own life. Born in the small qasba of Dibai, in Uttar Pradesh, Husain migrated to Pakistan in 1947. This radical transition forced Husain, an aspiring literary critic, into writing stories through which he hoped to fathom the meaning of existence and the myriad ways in which external events exert themselves upon existence. Husain's narrative journey evinces his lifelong engagement with questions thrown up by the Partition and his subsequent migration, as he admitted in one of his interviews, 'Explaining the experience of migration intellectually is a difficult task for me. I have been attempting to comprehend this experience through my stories.'[1] To Husain, storytelling was a journey, a quest, a spiritual experience or drawing from

---

1   Bruce R. Pray, trans., 'A Conversation between Intizar Husain and Muhammad Umar Memon,' *Journal of South Asian Literature* 18, 2 (1983): 165.

Sufi traditions, what he chose to term as *Varidat*. Speaking of the indispensability of stories for understanding human experiences, Charles E. Winquist writes, 'Without a story we are bound to the immediacy of the moment, and we are forever losing our grip on the reality of our own identity with the passage of discrete moments. We are unable to speak of primordial or eschatological time.'[2] Husain opted for the genre for it allowed him to understand the chaos and the commotion around him.

Partition and the spurious cultural geography it produced made a sensitive writer like Intizar Husain profoundly cognizant of his role as a writer, which was to remind his generation of its losses and instill some wisdom in the process. This choice, however, was not without challenges. 'To write poetry after Auschwitz is barbaric,'[3] wrote Theodor Adorno. Embedded in Husain's choice to write stories in order to make sense of the chaos around, were similar complex, ethical questions that urged for answers. Intrigued, Husain forged his own path on his creative journey.

A sceptic Husain eschewed formulaic rendering of events like progressives, which he considered vulgar. He rather chose to deal with events, howsoever despairing, head-on without glossing them over. He channelised his energies to comprehend experiences by placing them in their historical perspective.

---

2   Charles E. Winquist, 'The Act of Storytelling and the Self's Homecoming,' *Journal of the American Academy of Religion* 42, 1 (Mar. 1974): 103.

3   Theodor W. Adorno, 'Cultural Criticism and Society,' translated by Samuel Weber and Sherry Weber Nicholson in *Can One Live After Auschwitz?: A Philosophical Reader*, ed. Rolf Tiedemann, trans. Rodney Livingstone et al. Stanford: Stanford University Press, 2003), p. 162.

> I wanted to find out how and why all this is
> happening. In my attempt to trace back our history,
> I began to read history books...It is through my
> stories that I try to reach an understanding of
> what happened in 1947, in its own terms and
> against the background of those other migrations
> which have occurred in the history of Muslims.[4]

To Husain, if turning away from the past implied ignorance,
remembering it selectively or total surrender to it, in
exclusion of the immediate present, was no less vulgar, as
he wrote, 'It is a continuing tragedy of our history that we
never managed to bring about a synthesis of the old and
the new ways of thought. We either become completely
modern, intent on forgetting our history, our tradition or
we become reactionaries who shun the fresh breezes of new
ideas and knowledge which are all about us.'[5] Past, to Husain,
was necessary to illuminate the present, even if by its sheer
absence or unreachability. It intensified an awareness of the
present and prepared one for the journey ahead. Written
retrospectively, all Husain's works open prospectively.
Accused of being decadent for turning to the past, both
personal and communal, Husain always retorted, 'I am
trying to understand my history in terms of what is going
around me and in terms of those problems which affect us
as a community.'[6]

---

4   Pray, 'A Conversation between Intizar Husain and Muhammad Umar
     Memon,' *Journal of South Asian Literature* 18, 2 (1983): 165.

5   Ibid. p. 157.

6   Ibid. p. 159.

Intizar Husain's stories weave a rich tapestry of dreamlike surreal existence, around people, places, trees, birds, forests, bastis, flowers, temples, dargahs, imambaras, and other banal aspects of ordinary lives. Baffled by this banality, his critics are quick to castigate him for elements like nostalgia, attempts at retrieval of a lost world, and even passivity born out of Husain's Shia world view. However, one only needs to step back and consider Husain's entire fictional world to reckon that events and characters drawn from his past lives may or may not be a retrieval of his childhood days spent in his basti in pre-Partition India; they may or may not be an expression of nostalgia or a longing to go back to the lost world or even attempts to enlighten path for future based on an understanding of the past; in fact they may or may not even have any link to the lived experiences of the author. In Husain's fiction these questions have been rendered irrelevant, given the writer's engagement with deeper and immensely convoluted moral universe of the modern man. A 'vernacular cosmopolitan',[7] Husain's explorations into the local, native, and personal are guided by his quest for the universal.

The two novellas presented here delve into the ethical questions raised by the violent event of the Partition by turning to the past and situating the personal experience in historical perspective. They follow two different routes to come to terms with the cataclysmic events of the Partition. While *Din*, the story of Zamir and Tahsina and their repressed

---

7   See Homi Bhabha, 'The Vernacular Cosmopolitan,' in *Voices of the Crossing: The Impact of Britain on Writers from Asia, the Caribbean and Africa,* ed.Ferdinand Dennis and Naseem Khan (London: Serpent's Tail, 2000), pp. 133–142.

emotions, captures the personal past in all its drudgery and banality, *Dastan* moves beyond the personal to the realm of the historical and communal memory. Both these novellas capture Husain's unflinching faith in storytelling as a means of coming to grips with chaotic realities.

The Aesthetics of the Banal

Husain debunked the notion of anything like 'Islamic culture'. He rather upheld 'Indian Muslim Culture' which he thought was best exemplified in Hazrat Nizamuddin Aulia and Amir Khusro, a culture that was a product of years of living together in India with Hindus and assimilating many of their practices. He was pained to see this culture getting lost to Pakistan, a Muslim nation, under the influence of purists. In *Din*, he retrieves this culture in all its ethnographic details. The afternoon escapades of Zamir and Tahsina through the Kunjdon wali gali, qasai ki gali, and thatheri wali gali, beyond the Lal Mandir, Anjanharis, khandal trees, colour-changing chameleons, and countless other insects, flowers, and trees are conjured to life in vivid details. In the midst of all this unfolds the human drama of a growing intimacy between Zamir and Tahsina, Ammi's acerbic disapproval, Tai Amma's family anecdotes, the leisurely gossips of Badi Apa, Tai Amma and Ammi, the uneventful life of Hira and Gandal, the lawsuit concerning the haveli, Baba's decision to build a new kothi, and the eventual shifting of the residents of the haveli to this kothi followed by Badi Apa's stubborn refusal to shift. The novella abounds in such enervating details of the daily and the mundane that at times the reader feels suffocated, much like the characters in the novella, struggling with the pankha on sultry days when the wind is still. However, Husain believed that it is only by struggling through the quotidian that the short story writer arrives at the truth, 'The short story writer arrives at some truth—some awareness only after slogging through all the monotony and boredom of life and through all the realities surrounding him.'[8] Husain transforms the banal and the eventless into an aesthetic principle.

The narrative voice keeps shifting between the first person and the third person, blurring the distance between the omnipresent narrator and the protagonist Zamir. This deliberate ambiguity allows the authorial self to merge in the character and lends an autobiographical touch to the narrative, even as the author remains noncommittal and distant. Incidentally, the choice of the protagonist's name Zamir, meaning 'conscience', also hints at the inwardness of the story.[9]

As the adolescent Zamir journeys back to his basti along with his Baba and Ammi after receiving the news of his grandfather's demise, he is overwhelmed by the memories of the past—his childhood spent in his ancestral haveli, his memories of his affectionate but authoritarian grandfather,

---

8   Pray, 'A Conversation between Intizar Husain and Muhammad Umar Memon,' *Journal of South Asian Literature* 18, 2 (1983): 171.

9   Though Intizar Husain carefully chooses names of his protagonists in the context of his narratives, critics tend to over-interpret it. Zakir, the central character in the novel *Basti*, a history teacher, has been interpreted as a typically Shia name by some critics. However, Zakir is a common Muslim name, less so a Shia name. Zakir Naik, a controversial salafist preacher, and Zakir Hussain, the first Muslim president of India, are quick examples, while there are hardly any prominent Zakirs among Shias. It is an overly popular name in Bangladesh, a predominantly Sunni country.

his loving paternal aunt, his tender emotional bonding with his cousin Tahsina, and his distant observations of the nationalist politics, wherein the entire town including Abba Mian (who disapproved of Ali Brothers' support to Ibn-Saud) and Baba bemoaned the death of the Khilafat leader, Maulana Mohammad Ali. This past collides with the narrative present as the family arrives in the haveli. Zamir's modern, English-educated father opts for voluntary retirement and decides to build a modern-style kothi. Zamir becomes a witness to this painful transition marking the erosion of the old world. Even as Zamir and Tahsina experience the first flowering of adolescent love, they fail to articulate it. Constantly under the watchful gaze of their elders, they resign to the prevailing moral order. Steeped in an acute sense of dislocation, the overpowering code of morality which the majority of the characters adhere to, the novella has been accused of being soaked in despair, hopelessness, and obsessed with the world of dead people. 'This acceptance of the tyranny of the mundane is horrifying,'[10] writes one critic.

Intizar Husain, however, remained undeterred by these charges. In a note titled 'About My Characters,' he underscores the futility of this idea: ,Had Tehsina wept, what would she have got, or Zamir, what would he have achieved had he declared himself?' He goes on to add, 'I did not advise them at all in the matter. Zamir's decision is quite his own. I had no say in the matter. I am not Zamir.'[11]In the overarching logic

---

10   Waqas Khwaja, 'The Lost World of Intizar Husain,' NP. Web. DoA 3/05/2007.

11   Intizar Husain, Apney Kirdaron Key Barey Mein,' in *Janam Kahanian* (Lahore: Sang-e-meel, 1987), p. 751. Cited in Waqas Khwaja, Ibid.

of the novel, individuals like Zamir, Tahsina, and others do not matter as much as their situations. The characters of the novel are victims of their situations. Like other writings of Intizar Husain, the novella too refrains from making any direct reference to the Partition and the trauma of migration, but it does deal with a world changed by it.

Intizar Husain is interested in mapping the ethical anxieties of the human conscience located in a morally debilitating universe. In his essay 'Literature and Love',[12] Husain speaks of war and political instability having a direct impact on the ability to love. He feels that unlike pre-1857 when love was a full-time engagement, Urdu literature of the colonial period succumbed to Victorian morality. In Husain's view, the subordination of love to morality is as much of an immoral act as the immorality of segregation of sorrow born out of political turmoil from the personal sorrow. He idealises Mir in whose poetry 'personal sorrows and the sorrows of the age dissolved into one and all sorrows, when blended into one, became the sorrow of love'.[13] In the same vein, the pervasive note of sorrow in the novella can be seen as an outcome of the atmosphere of political turmoil and the novelist's own sense of dislocation. The protagonist's urge to shed the burden of the past and fix his mind on the journey ahead is symptomatic of this split between the lyrical emotion of love ['gham-e-mohabbat'] and the banal ['gham-i-rozgar']. The banality and the suffering and wretchedness

---

12   Intizar Husain, 'Literature and Love' in *Story is a Vagabond: Fiction, Essays and Drama by Intizar Husain*, ed. Alok Bhalla, Asif Farrukhi, and Nishat Zaidi, *Manoa* 27:1, pp. 220–225.

13   Ibid., p. 223.

of characters is an outcome of the horrors of the Partition and a decline in humanist traditions. At the core of it lies the loss of meaning. The narrative's engagement with Zamir's mind, which is a ragbag of poetic images surrounding his tender romantic encounters with Tahsina, contradicts its other—the banal or the mundane, wherein Zamir must leave to find employment, manipulated through his father's connection, and make a living. Husain refuses to relieve the everyday with the dramatic, or allow the trivial to become an object of reverence, in the manner of myths and legends, by infusing any elevated sermon or lesson into his story.

Possibilities of Conversation between the Human and the Non-Human

The ethical question in Husain's stories is not anthropocentrically framed, but rather encompasses the flora and the fauna, the entire landscape, and all things living and dead. The ecosystem exists contiguously with the human world. It is not a metaphor. Human and non-human agents are part of one scene, wherein they exist separately and yet act upon each other, forming one syntagm.

In his essay 'Vikram, the Vampire and the Story', Husain argues that 'in a world containing only people, there is room for journalism to grow but not for poems and stories'.[14] He laments the fact that unlike ancient stories which thrived on communication between the human and the non-human, and in which man appeared as part of the universe, the new-age storyteller 'began to write tales of only the human

---

14   Intizar Husain, 'Vikram, the Vampire and the Story' in *Story is a Vagabond: Fiction, Essays and Drama by Intizar Husain, Manoa* 27:1, p. 241.

world'.[15] The tragic outcome of this loss of the non-human is that man himself has metamorphosed into a demon. The loss of the ability to listen to stories with wonderment is the greatest tragedy of modern man.

In the narrative of *Din*, the life in a qasba is magically recreated without turning the attention away from the story. The story is achingly mired in quotidian details. However, the ordinary becomes enchanting when seen through the childhood gaze of Zamir and Tahsina. For instance:

> Passing through the temple lane, he was filled with awe. The red-stone temple radiated heat from a distance. It always mystified him. He wondered who lived in it, human beings or djinns; who blew the conch shells, played the cymbals and rang the bells at day break and again at dusk. High above, attached to a tiny window, there was an iron pulley which remained at rest during the day, but the moment the sun set, it began to turn on its own; and a bright polished brass pot, attached to a white rope, descended from the window and fell into the dark well with a splash, as though someone had spun gold coins chiming and ringing through the air. After a while, sparkling with overflowing water, it resurfaced, ascended to the window and suddenly vanished. Who released the rope down the pulley, who pulled it up, and where did it come from?

---

15   Intizar Husain, 'Vikram, the Vampire and the Story' in *Story is a Vagabond: Fiction, Essays and Drama by Intizar Husain*, Editors, *Manoa* 27:1, p. 243.

Zamir and Tahsina, and later Achhe and Bunni, sending their salams to Allah Mian through the butterflies, the bees, the mud lanes, the vacant buildings, dense trees, the neem flowers, and birds nesting in the neem tree, the stories of Tai Amma about Amils and faqirs, are all part of the story and constituent of the temporality of the narrative.

The presence of the non-human is more pronounced in the second novella *Dastan*, which follows the pattern of a traditional dastan. It has a mysterious black river which forces gallants to jump into its dark waters, a throbbing desert and a rotating tower, an empty city with vacant houses, faqirs who appear and disappear mysteriously, a horse whose neighing foretells events, a parrot that shows directions, etc. The novella is replete with such references to the non-human world that co-exists with the human world and interacts with them. Tote Mian lives in the midst of parrots. When he relates the story of his youth, he describes how he spent his youthful days flying pigeons. Tote Mian's Amil father echoes the sentiments of Intizar Husain, when he warns him:

> Forests are cut down and cities are built; cities are destroyed and forests regrow. Everyone mourns for cities which are now desolate; but friends, take care to also recall those forests which were cut down to build cities. What happened to those tall trees? Each tree was a city, each leaf a neighbourhood, each bud a lane. Vanished!

To Husain, cutting down of a tree was no less of a tragedy than the loss of a human life. After the Partition, when he migrated to Lahore, he experienced the loss of home not only in terms of friends and folks left behind but also in terms of tamarind trees, birds, fruits, flora, and fauna that were a part of the scene he left behind in his basti. Husain's resolve to write stories is rooted in his resolve to retrieve those trees, and not let them wither. He says, '…why do I persist in writing my stories? Perhaps because a neem tree was once outside me and a neem tree is still inside me. Whatever may have happened to the outer tree, let the inner core not wither. My commitment is to my neem tree, with its bitter fruit. 'Cling to the tree,' to the neem tree and to the stories, 'without any hope of spring'.[16]

Husain does cling to his commitment by telling stories, and telling them well. He does not adulterate his stories with a message or a lesson, much like his inspiration, Gautama Buddha, who told stories of his past lives as birds, animals, or trees, and never used them to preach or sermonise.

Between the Fantastical and the Real

Unlike *Din* which delves into the personal past and uses ethnomethodology in its efforts to make sense of the chaotic reality, *Dastan* connects disparate temporalities and spaces and blurs the line between the real and the fantastic, or history and fiction. Written in the classical prose of the dastan tradition, the frame narrative here consists of people displaced by *fasad* (riots).[17] Hakim Ji's entire library of dastans

---

16   Intizar Husain, 'Vikram, the Vampire and the Story' in *Story is a Vagabond: Fiction Essays and Drama by Intizar Husain, Manoa* 27:1, p. 244.

17   The novella does not specifically mention the period when these riots took place, thus circumventing a direct reference to the Partition and leaving a silhouette of ambiguity.

was burnt in those riots. Thus, the riots caused the loss not just of lives and property, but also of stories. Bereft of their stories, the characters wander without direction. However, with some effort, Hakim Ji does manage to recall a few of these stories he claims are not fantastical but real: 'In Hakim Ji's mind, the thin line which separates a dastan from reality was almost obliterated. Countless people and incidents from his dastans seemed and felt real and while so many real incidents receded into fiction.'

Written in two parts, 'Jal Garje' [The Thunder of Rivers] and 'Ghode Ki Nida' [The Scream of the Horse], the novella, with its embellished, lyrical prose, has layers of stories moving backward in time, each providing a context to the other, illuminating the frame narrative and in turn illuminated by it. In the frame narration of the first part, Samand Khan takes us through a world where historical facts, legends, and the fantastical collide into each other: the desolation of the rebel soldiers of 1857 lead by Bakht Khan, the legend of Sher Shah Suri's fantastic tower in the middle of a desert that once throbbed like a heart, the dark and mysterious black river whose waters roared like thunder, and beyond this a desolate city with deserted streets and houses and palaces in ruins. Similarly, Tote Mian, the narrator of the frame narrative of the second part, takes us through his youth when his mother saw a blood-dripping Alam in her dreams, and had a premonition of the impending tragedy. His Amil father told him the legend of the 'riderless' horse of Imam Husain that is awaiting a rider who would end the atrocities and injustices. The horse is the cause of Haider Ali's success. Tipu Sultan's fall is attributed to his failure to recite Naad-i-Ali (a prayer, calling Hazrat Ali for help) before climbing this horse.

Throughout the novella, facts and historical events are woven into the essential threads of the dastan,[18] that is, *Razm* (war), *Bazm* (assembly), *Husn-o-Ishq* (beauty and love), and *Tilism* (enchantment). The episodes of Samand Khan sleeping with Gulshan-i-khoobi with a naked sword between them or Tote Mian's liaison with Shahzadi Mahal are also in conformity with the dastan convention. Formulaic openings, interminable wanderings, fabulous characters, and many more such elements that defy the 'logic of causality'[19] aim at interrogating the nature of the real, for, as Husain would say, 'The external world possesses a type of reality for me, but I want to know, what lies behind that reality, what are the sources of that reality.'[20]

In the enchanted world of a traditional dastan, 'nothing is what it seems',[21] and the protagonist has to break the

18   The Persio-Arabic tradition of dastan travelled to India and Urdu has a rich tradition of dastan. For instance eight Daftars of *Dastan-i-Amir Hamza* published by Naval Kishore Press between 1881-1917, Rajab Ali Beg Suroor's *Fasana-i-Ajaib* published by Naval Kishore Press in 1867, Mir Amman's *Bagh-o-Bahar etc.*, For more on dastan see, Frances Pritchett, *The Medieval Persian Romance Tradition* (New York: Columbia University Press, 1991), Shamsur Rahman Faruqi's *Amir Hamzatzubani Bayaniya, Bayankunina, aur Samaiin* (New Delhi: Maktaba Jamia, 1998); *Sahiri, Shahi, Sahibqirani: Dastan-i-Amir Hamza Ka Mutalaba'a* (Delhi: Qaumi Kauncil Barai-Farogh-i-Urdu Zuban, 1999), and Gyan Chandra Jain's *Urdu ki Nasri Dastanein.* (2nd ed. (Karachi: Anjuman-e Taraqqi-e Urdu, 1969). Musharraf Ali Farooqi, 'The Simurgh-Feather Guide to the Poetics of Dastan-e Amir Hamza Sahibqiran,' in *The Annual of Urdu Studies*, 15:1 (2000): 119–167.

19   '... instead of the Law of Causality, it [a dastan] is subject to Law of Possibility.' Shamsur Rahman Faruqi is cited in Musharraf Ali Farooqi, 'The Simurgh-Feather Guide,' ibid., p. 135.

20   Pray, 'A Conversation between Intizar Husain and Muhammad Umar Memon,' *Journal of South Asian Literature* 18, 2 (1983): 160.

21   Frances W. Pritchett, '*Amir Hamza*' in *South Asian Folklore An Encyclopaedia*, ed. Margaret A. Mills, Peter J Claus, and Sarah Diamond (New York & London: Routledge, 2003), p.15.

tilism, kill the magician before he can return to the normative narrative space and time. Underlying this world of ajaib and gharaib is the Sufi philosophy that views this universe as an illusion, a tilism. This structure of freely flowing imaginative narrative, with no moral obligation, and marked by humour and optimism is replaced in Husain's dastan by an overarching sense of fear and suspense, by a sense of foreboding, and a looming tragedy. The traditional dastan plunges the reader into a universe of infinite possibilities, of unbridled emotions, an ever-expanding world of sights and sounds, and rids him/her of all feeling of powerlessness or helplessness. In Husain's dastan, however, the reader is deprived of this redemptive transformation, as the heroes (of dastan) as well as the reader/listener remain bewildered at the end of their adventure. The rich descriptions, enchanting details, and fantastic exaggerations woven in a language that is given to excessive verbiage and internally rhyming sentences do not lead to the revelation of a sign as such in Husain's novella. Although the adventurous journey of the hero of a conventional dastan marks a release from reality, his return to the normative narrative is accompanied by a new knowledge which sharpens his and the reader's perception of reality. It facilitates a firmer grip on reality. However, for the heroes in Husain's dastan, no such solace is available. They either get killed in their adventurous expedition or lose their moorings and end up spending their days in anonymity like Tote Mian or the faqir of Hakim Ji's dastans. Akin to a traditional dastan, Husain's dastan too evades an organic ending with Ghani dreaming of the sound of the galloping horse which inspired generations of people to take up arms against oppression.

Abandoning the world of evincible logic, Intizar Husain here moves to construe Islamic history as a continuum by tracing back the present moment of post-Partition crisis marked by migration and homelessness, to the desolation of rebel soldiers of 1857 lead by Bakht Khan, anti-British battles of Haider Ali and Tipu Sultan, the glorious reign of Shershah, and finally back to the martyrdom of Imam Husain in the battle of Karbala. The figure that links all these stories together is the figure of the riderless horse of slain Imam Husain. Having disappeared after the Imam's death, the horse reappears recurrently across the various times and locations to aid the brave men in their fight against injustice. This seems like Husain's ostensible attempt at conceptualising a history of the subcontinent Muslims in Islamic or rather Shia terms. Husain concurred with this possibility when he said, 'When I came to Pakistan and felt myself to be a Pakistani, I was thinking as a Pakistani.'[22] In fact, this is further borne out by the fact that 'Ghode ki Nida' (The Scream of the Horse) was written to commemorate the centenary celebration of 1857 and was first published in *Naya Daur* (v. 11–12: 19–45) in about 1958 or 1959. However, a closer attention makes it evident that far from resurrecting a monochromatic, singular past, Husain, by locating this view of history in the realm of the fantastic, underlines an inherent futility of this vision.

Conclusion

The two novellas may appear to be diametrically opposed to each other—one steeped in the nostalgia of a personal past,

---

22   Asif Farrukhi, 'Talking about *Basti*: Intizar Husain in Conversation with Asif Farrukhi,' Lahore 2005. Web. DoA 12/04/2007. http://www.columbia. edu/itc/mealac/pritchett/00litlinks/basti/00_background.html.

the other randomly moving from the historical to fantastic; one marked by a colloquial language rooted in the local and the other written in high style, elite [*Ashraf*], classical idiom; one marked by eventlessness, the other following a narrative style that is inextricably event-bound. However, like Milan Kundera's character Sabina in the novel, *The Unbearable Lightness of Being*, who explains her paintings to Tereza, 'On the surface the intelligible lie; underneath an unintelligible truth showing through',[23] Intizar Husain also paints the phenomenal world only to peer through its illusions to reveal what is hidden beneath. By clothing experience in the language of myths and legends, and putting language to it ontological use, Husain's stories, even when they relate a sense of futility and nothingness, are a positive affirmation of the act of storytelling. This manifests, what Winquist calls, 'an active response to the desire to know'.[24] It is this that makes Husain a thoroughly modern writer.

Traversing at the cusp of two identities, a Pakistani national and an Indian migrant, Hussain's fiction dwells on the futility of identity politics, and undergirds the need for intersubjective accommodations. His stories, ranging from the personal to the political, the local to the mythic, the individual to the communal draw from a wide range of narrative traditions such as Western traditions of Kafka, Indo-Persian *Dastan*, Buddhist *Jatakas*, and the Sanskrit *Panchatantra* and *Singhasan Batisi*. They debunk the

---

23 Milan Kundera, *The Unbearable Lightness of Being*, trans. Michael Henry Heim (London: Faber and Faber, 1985), pp. 63–64.

24 Charles E. Winquist, 'The Act of Storytelling and the Self's Homecoming,' *Journal of the American Academy of Religion* 42, 1 (Mar. 1974): 104.

anthropomorphism of the Habermasian communicative rationality, social realism of the Marxist Progressives, symbolism of his contemporary Urdu writers, and uphold identity as 'beholden and responsible first and foremost to the other'.[25]

By simultaneously engaging with local culture, nationalist politics, and universal ethics, Husain's fiction exemplifies the best in the world literature.

---

25 Jeffrey Thomas Nealon, *Alterity Politics: Ethics and Performative Subjectivity* (Durham: Duke University Press, 1998), p. 4.

DAY

One

The past was, for him, a sequence of long nights and scorching afternoons. In between, an odd wet morning or a rain-drenched day seemed like a precious pearl. His days were spent rambling from lane to lane and field to field. His nights were blank and meaningless. He was like a drifter. When he was awake, he heard stories. When he slept, he wandered in his dreams, but he did not know how far he had come or how much further he still had to go. At night, when the entire haveli was asleep, and the streets outside simmered in silence, Mir Bu Ali's groans could be heard from quite a distance.

Next to the haveli was a semi-concrete kothari with an open courtyard. All through winter, summer, and rain, Mir Bu Ali slept under the open sky, or rather groaned and sighed. During the few nights, when it rained or drizzled, and Mir Bu Ali slept under the roof of the kothari, the sequence of snores, snorts, and hiccups became so loud and prolonged that the entire mohalla would wake up. In his sleep, Mir Bu

Ali screamed wild prophecies which somehow turned out to be true.

One night, at first he whimpered, but then began to scream, 'He has gone, he has gone.' In the morning, news arrived that there had been a robbery in Kankadkheda. Tai Amma informed us that, since the time Mir Bu Ali's Jalali Wazifa had gone wrong, his hamzad was uncontrollable and did not let him sleep at night. Zamir and Tahsina were always alarmed at the mention of Jalali Wazifa and hamzad. Tai Amma was herself bewildered. All she knew was that on the fortieth night of the ritual, Mir Bu Ali began to scream in his kothari, 'It has fallen, it has fallen!' Then he banged at the gate of the haveli. Bade Abba was still alive and used to pray the whole night. He quietly got up from his prayer-mat and opened the gate. Mir Bu Ali continued to bang at the gate and scream, 'It has fallen, it has fallen!' Irritated, Bade Abba glared at him and asked, 'What has fallen?' Terrified, Mir Bu Ali replied, 'The roof.' Ever since that day, he hasn't had the good fortune to sleep under a roof. Whenever he slept under a roof, he whimpered, screamed, and disturbed the sleep of the entire mohalla. The next day, when the sun rose, he looked like a corpse; no screaming, no groaning, not a word to anyone. He merely sat on a string cot like a bundle all day and dozed. Zamir and Tahsina stood outside the courtyard and watched him in fear and awe for hours, and then quietly slipped away.

And then, there was Gadhhe Shah. Only Tai Amma had seen him. Mir Bu Ali was real; Zamir and Tahsina had seen him with their own eyes; Gadhhe Shah was a legend, narrated by Tai Amma. A fervent devotee, Gadhhe Shah had built a shelter by the boundary wall of the haveli. He sat there all day digging a pit with his hands, and if someone asked, he'd reply, 'This fakir is building a house to live in.' When the pit became deeper, he sat inside it. One day Bade Abba went up to him and pleaded, 'Shahji, the haveli is at your disposal. Please come inside.' Gadhhe Shah responded indifferently, 'The haveli is under the ground.' Offended, Bade Abba reacted sharply, 'Then go live underground.' The next day, there was no sign either of Gadhhe Shah or the pit.

Zamir and Tahsina listened and wondered. Tai Amma quietly marvelled at the story for some time. Then, breaking her silence, said, 'Our Abba was a renowned Amil. In fact, Bhaiyya, ours is a family of Amils. In those days there was always an Amil in each generation. But that tradition ended with Bade Abba.'

'Why?'

'There was no one to succeed him. Abba Mian's pursuits were different. And because he never paid any attention to his father's knowledge, it was passed on to others. It so happened that when Bade Abba took to bed, a naked fakir appeared from somewhere. He pitched his tent in front of the haveli. Bade Abba's condition continued to deteriorate and he was on the verge of death. For three days he was in a bad shape; he gasped for breath; he was in such pain that only Allah could help. Bibi, it so happened that on the third day, that stark-naked ascetic, stout and well-built like a bull, barged into our house. Women began to scream, but Bade Abba signalled to let him in. Everyone was shocked. Ai Bibi, he went straight to Bade Abba and embraced him. Bade Abba shivered and...died...the fakir left. And, then, the fakir disappeared. People searched and searched for him, but there was no trace of him. Ever since then, there has been no Amil in the haveli.... '

Memories of family elders, anecdotes, stories of djinns and ghosts, or some other tale—Tai Amma's dastans never ended. When the night was wet with dew, Zamir's eyes, heavy with sleep, slowly closed; and when he woke up again, others were asleep; silence, darkness; snores; the sound of Mir Bu Ali's groans seemed to come from the edge of dreams. Zamir's heart pounded with fear and his teeth chattered in the cold; suddenly, he discovered that he was not on his cot, but on Badi Apa's cot; he slowly snuggled close to her warm, plump body; her loving bosom lulled him back to sleep. When he opened his eyes again, he woke to the same silence, darkness, and sounds of someone snoring; he saw dark paths ahead and dark paths behind; no friend, no companion; sleep deserted him; he no longer heard Mir Ali groan from the edge of dreams. He lay awake as the night grew longer; as he felt suffocated, he threw aside the warm quilt covering his body, and stared wide-eyed into the darkness. Suddenly, the sound of the azan floated in like a ray of sunlight in the darkness. He was relieved that the night was about to end; then, the Lal Mandir came into life with conch shells, clashing cymbals, and chiming bells; a whirlpool of light slowly emerged from the darkness, spread, and then faded away; there was silence once more as though the night, which was about to end, had returned. In the encircling darkness, he felt suffocated again; but, then, he heard the sound of looms from the cotton mill; the sound of one loom, and then, after a pause, another, and then another, forming a string of sounds, like a stream of light breaking through a wall of darkness; a jarring noise, followed by a thin whirring sound of something spinning; the sound of a loom which whistled like a stranded railway engine; and, then a sound which was heavier, harsher, and longer; it was the longest dirge of the night, and he thought it would never end; but, it too slowly faded; it was the last lament of the night; the cotton mill fell silent after that. The cotton mill was also the last signpost of his afternoon wanderings; when he reached it, he stared in wonder at its tall, sturdy, red-brick chimneys which seemed to reach for the sky; they marked the boundary of some alien land; he watched them from afar and then returned. Everyone was still asleep when he woke up again.

In the afternoons, when the air was still and suffocating, or the sun was scorching, or a hot dust storm brought countless miseries, Zamir either lazed under the shade of trees, or wandered across the blazing barren land, or roamed through green fields; he walked and walked till his legs ached; Tahsina's fair face turned red and a few strands of hair clung to her ears and neck drenched in sweat. On their way back home, they walked through the temple lane and from the temple lane to the lane with a water-tank, where they washed their hands, feet, and faces, before turning into their own lane. Passing through the temple lane, he was filled with awe. The red stone temple radiated heat from a distance. It always mystified him. He wondered who lived in it, human beings or djinns; who blew the conch shells, played the cymbals, and rang the bells at daybreak and again at dusk. High above, attached to a tiny window, there was an iron pulley which remained at rest during the day, but the moment the sun set, it began to turn on its own; and a bright polished brass pot, attached to a white rope, descended from the window and fell into the dark well with a splash, as though someone had spun gold coins chiming and ringing through the air. After a while, sparkling with overflowing water, it resurfaced, ascended to the window, and suddenly vanished. Who released the rope down the pulley, who pulled it up, and where did it come from? The thread of his thoughts became longer and longer till he lost hold of it. Soon, a wasp, hovering over a shallow pool of water near the stone slab of the well, caught his attention. The red stone slab was so hot in the sun that his feet burnt the moment he stepped on it. But, all year round, there were pools of water nearby; a lone dragonfly circled above the surface of a pool; an anjanhari, with golden patches and black spots, came down to the edge of a pool, buzzed, and flew away. Beyond the temple lane, the water-tank lane offered shade throughout the afternoon, and the water-kiosk was always open. After drinking water, both Zamir and Tahsina stood in a pool of cool water which, though clean, was stained with a layer of green scum. As they stood in it, cold water flowed over their feet. One day, while standing there, Zamir slipped and his knees were badly bruised. Tahsina burst out laughing. Zamir was on the brink of tears, but he controlled himself. He was annoyed with Tahsina for a long time after that. When he reached the khandal tree, he broke off a green, supple sprig, but refused to give it to Tahsina.

'Zamir, give me that sprig,' Tahsina asked longingly.

'Why should I?' He dryly replied.

'Please, I'll give you the blue crystal in exchange when we get home,' she implored.

'Who cares for the blue crystal? I won't give you this.'

Upset, Tahsina did not plead again. She began to climb the tree herself. As she climbed higher and higher, he kept taunting her. Whenever she lost her balance, he mocked, 'There you go.' But she always regained her balance. She reached a large branch and stood on it to break a sprig. The wind was blowing hard; in a strong gust of wind, strands of her dry, golden hair fell over her face, and her loose white pyjamas, which she had worn that morning for the first time, lifted. Suddenly, there was another gust of wind. He felt as if lightening had flashed across his brain. He shouted, 'Tahsina is naked.' Tahsina, who was plucking the sprig, froze. Her legs trembled a bit, but she regained control, and quietly came down. Her brows were arched like two bows, her lips were tightly shut, her face was red, and her eyes were burning with rage; he was transfixed when he saw her. She walked towards him slowly. He stood motionless, unable to move; his heart pounded loudly. As she came closer, he was frightened to death. But Tahsina's fire-spitting eyes had welled up with tears. Crying inconsolably, she turned and ran home.

Zamir's feet were heavy and his heart sank. Lost, he stood beside the well for hours.

As Hira pulled up pots of water with all his strength and placed them near his feet, he sang loudly: 'O ji, Ganga, Jamuna, Saraswati, seven sisters of Indus, flow!'

Clear, colourless drops of water fell on Hira's fair, cracked feet; flowed into the rock pool and from the rock pool into a muddy drain. Zamir stood watching for a long time and then walked away.

He paused at the door of his house. He was in deep thought, wondering if he should go inside. Nervous, he pushed the gate open, crossed the outer courtyard, entered the inner courtyard surreptitiously, and peeped through the chink in the door. Though he couldn't see anything, he heard Abba Mian shouting. 'Perhaps, Tahsina has complained to Abba Mian,' he thought and his heart began to beat loudly. He quickly retreated and stepped back into the lane again. Only when he reached the temple, did he look back. Someone was coming. He felt more at ease and slowed down. A dragonfly was hovering over a tiny pool. The sun was going down, but the women had not yet gathered at the well to collect water. Suddenly, the dormant pulley near the window of the temple came to life. A brightly burnished pot began to descend. The rope became longer and longer; and the pot continued its decent until it fell with a splash into the well. A little later, the long rope was pulled up; it vanished into the window. The golden pot, spilling pearl-like droplets of water, also disappeared into the dark room. He was mystified once again. He stared at the quiet pulley for long, trying to resolve the riddle of that mysterious window. A wasp distracted his attention. He waved his hands wildly to drive it away. It flew back to the pool of water where many more yellow wasps were hovering. They reminded him of that sprig which he had dropped under the khandal tree. If he still had it with him, he could have driven them away. Reminded of the entire incident, his heart ached. Sad and gloomy, he began to walk. He was thirsty again as he passed

the water tank. He scooped up water in his palms and drank.
The water was warm and tasteless. His mouth was still dry
and thirst still unquenched. From the water tank he came to
the street where, after sunset, many street vendors sold chaat
on pushcarts. A hungry dog stood in a corner, its gaze fixed
on the food. As soon as a customer threw away a leaf-plate
after eating dahi-bada, the dog leapt forward to lick it.

The shops in the bazaar were familiar. He had often
stood before them for hours admiring images of Ravana,
the ten-headed demon, or gazing at Hanumanji, the Monkey
God, flying over Lanka as it burnt, or wondering why the
black-hooded snake, wrapped around Shivji's neck, never
hissed at Shivji himself. He went to each one of those shops,
stood before them, and then listlessly moved on. At last,
when the oil lamps with wicks were lit, he turned and walked
back home.

'Who is it? Zamir? Why are you standing in the dark?
Where have you been?'

He could no longer restrain the storm raging inside him;
his eyes overflowed with tears and he began to weep. Abba
Mian forgot his anger, hugged Zamir, and pulled him inside.

Zamir's memories of Abba Mian were still vivid but
fragmentary: his fair, broad, wrinkled ageing body, white
beard and hair; a slightly bent back; his white muslin
kurta; a tiny silver sword, which hung around his neck like
a pendant and which he used to pick his teeth with after
meals. When Abba Mian felt drowsy as he smoked his
huqqa, he would push its pipe away and stretch his back on
the hard wooden cot covered with a white sheet, rest his
white head on a bolster, and begin to snore. He would wake

up with a start and walk to the mosque for his zohr prayers. Tastefully crafted and carefully designed, red and grey chillums stood in neat rows in the alcove; the ones with beautifully carved lattice work were gifts. A large swinging cloth-fan, with frills, hung on hooks from the wooden beam of the high roof, remained in motion throughout the day, and stirred the air in every corner of the drawing room. A brass spittoon; a walking stick in the shape of Urdu letter 'Laam' stood in a corner; a broad wooden cot with a white sheet and a bolster. Abba Mian sat on that cot throughout the day. Visitors sat on stools, smoked the huqqa, chewed pan, chatted, and left. After the visitors left and the drawing room was empty, Abba Mian would drowsily call, 'Zamir, Tahsina, where are you?' Zamir and Tahsina would come running and hug Abba Mian. After all, he gave them an anna each every day. But Abba Mian's summons in the afternoons sometimes also carried a threat of imprisonment: 'The wind outside is dusty and hot. Go to sleep.' With Tahsina on one side and him on the other, Abba Mian lay in the middle and snored. Zamir and Tahsina would look at each other meaningfully. As they tried to quietly sneak out, the rhythm of Abba Mian's snores would break: 'Where are you going? Lie down.' Once again they would lie down flat, hold their breath, and wait with their eyes tightly shut. At the irresistible sound of the bell of the ice-cream vendor, they would jump off the bed, run to the street, and take out the one anna tucked in the belt of their pyjamas to buy ice cream. Slices of white ice cream frozen on green leaf-plates would begin to melt as soon as they touched them with their fingers. After they had finished licking their fingers, they would lick the leaf-plate. Then, afraid of Abba Mian, they would nervously return home.

They caught sight of a butterfly flitting through the veranda. Trying to catch it, they sprinted excitedly up the staircase. Tahsina caught it, held it between her fingers, stood near the parapet, and raising it to the sky, said, 'O butterfly, convey my salaam to Allah Mian.' 'And mine too,' he shouted eagerly. 'Why yours? This butterfly belongs to me. O butterfly! Convey Tahsina's salaam to Allah Mian.' Her fingers released the butterfly and fluttering in the wind, it flew away. Close to tears, at that moment, he hated Tahsina. Sad, he lingered on the dilapidated terrace covered with stubs of dried grass for a long time; he walked on the parapet or along the corridor which led to the big drain through which rainwater flowed down a tin pipe and fell with a loud splash into the lane below. Disconsolate, he turned to go down, when he spotted a tiny butterfly nestling in the rubble of a corridor destroyed by monkeys. 'I have caught a butterfly!' he screamed loudly. He too stood on the same parapet to send his message, 'Butterfly! Convey my salaam to Allah Mian!' Tahsina wistfully looked at his butterfly. When he released the butterfly, it floated down slowly and languidly in the sun-scorched wind. Tahsina shouted triumphantly, 'Your butterfly looks tired. How will it reach Allah Mian? Lo, it's floating down.' Suddenly, a gust of wind lifted it up again and the butterfly began to soar. They always quarrelled about sending messages to Allah Mian. After all, a butterfly could not convey more than one salaam at a time and Tahsina was selfish enough to send only hers to Allah Mian. Yet, when they heard the magical voice of Singi Bai, their hearts throbbed in concert and their nervous eyes revealed the same story. In fear, they huddled together near the wall close to the staircase and drew so close to each other that they could hear each other's heartbeats. They sat close to each other for a long time and then stuck their heads out to see if Singi Bai was still there in the lane or had left. A butterfly! They leapt up at the sight of a stray butterfly in the lane and, forgetting all about Singi Bai, shot down the staircase into the courtyard and from the courtyard into the lane. But the butterfly was nowhere to be found. Where had it gone? It had vanished. And they set out on a long and adventurous journey in search of butterflies, braving discoloured thorny scrubs, crooked acacia trees, black, rugged bushes with red berries, and beyond them a green khandal tree, a tall peepal tree, and many dense neem trees so entangled with each other that there was no sign of sunlight under them. On reaching those trees, often the destination of their journey changed. From butterflies, their minds turned to chameleons. Who knows how many chameleons were hidden in those trees. Every afternoon they ground at least one chameleon into paste; but, the next day when they went back again, they noticed in the hole of a neem trunk or in the branch of a khandal tree a few pink mouths or yellow tails. When they killed chameleons with a green, supple khandal branch or a stone, they thought they were taking revenge because a chameleon had once eaten a hole through the leather water bag of Hazrat Abbas. Later, they would walk up to the well nearby, wash their hands and feet, cup some water in their hands to drink, and sit with their feet soaking in the cold, clear pools of water which sparkled like pearls. They would watch the young and strong Hira sing as he pulled up brass pots filled with water from the well: 'O ji, Ganga, Jamuna, Saraswati, seven sisters of Indus, flow!' Countless white flowers, falling like torrential rain, scattered at his feet. Gandal, his dhoti tied above his dark knees, his thick moustache covering his lips, untied his bulls. 'Move, bloody bulls!' he swore and flogged the obstinate bulls till they ran up the slope once again and left a trail of dust behind. Zamir's heart pounded when he saw the bulls, afraid that they may stray from their path and charge towards him. Tahsina and he got up and walked back to the grove of trees and the chameleons. He was afraid of the chameleons, but the moment he sighted one, he could not help killing it. For a moment, he felt bloodthirsty. Only once did he fail to kill a chameleon. At that time, far from killing it, he couldn't even raise his hand. 'A chameleon!' Tahsina sharply tugged at his sleeve. Emerging from under the roots of a peepal tree, the chameleon was climbing up the trunk. The moment he picked up a stone, the chameleon paused, raised its head an inch above the trunk, and changed its colour to a smouldering red ember. It swelled to double its size; its neck and back were so red that it seemed to be in rage. Tahsina's hand gripped his arm more tightly. Their two hearts beat to the same rhythm, at the same pace. The two became one. Alone. There was no soul in sight for miles and no human sound; the pulley over the well seemed to have got stuck and no water splashed from the brass pot; and it appeared as if the bulls had suddenly stopped in their race down the slope. And Hira and Gandal had vanished; and there was no one near the well. Everything, every sound was still; their feet, their pounding hearts, the brick held in one hand, the roots of the peepal tree, and the supple khandal branch. Only the chameleon, twisting its body and flicking its tail, seemed to be alive. It changed its colour from red to green, as if it was melting into an intense wave of colours— swirling, angry, enraged waves of colour. Soon, another wave of colours swept through its body as it changed from green to blue. Zamir and Tahsina lost count of the colours and sense of time; no longer did they know where they were, or for how long they had been standing there; how many changes of colour they had watched and how many more they would see.

When they were finally able to move, they were startled to see a long yellow tail flicker and vanish under the peepal leaves. They were relieved and their hearts began to beat normally again. Their paralysed feet instinctively began to move towards the well where the pulley was turning as usual, and the cool, clear water splashed on Hira's feet and flowed into the stone pool, from the pools into the muddy drains, and from drains into fields. They quietly drank some water and walked back home—silent and pensive. Fear still cast its shadow over their eyes, and their hearts had yet not ceased to pound. The air was still and the bushes seemed to wilt in the sun. Suddenly, the earth gripped their feet. A few steps ahead, a gust of wind swirled up. 'A witch!' Tahsina cried and again clung to his arm. The whirling wind swept up pieces of paper, gathered strings of kites, dirty feathers of hens and pigeons, small pebbles, and swept them up into the sky.

When they got back home, Badi Apa reprimanded them, 'Where did you go? Look at your faces, they are red. Only fools go out when the wind is hot and dusty.'

Both of them remained silent. Though an aunt, Badi Apa was more than a mother to Zamir. Tahsina was her daughter, but Badi Apa loved him better. She bathed him, made him sleep with her, and when Baba decided to take him away, she was annoyed, displeased, and cursed Ammi. And when her pleas were ineffective, she wept. Baba also turned out to be a strong-willed person. He neither paid any attention to Abba Mian nor was he moved by Badi Apa's tears.

'Of course, Bhaiyya! He's your son. Your wife must have told you that Phuphi will spoil the boy. Take him away. Do as you please, Bhaiyya! Who am I to stop you?'

Badi Apa continued to taunt. Baba listened, but did not change his decision. Baba always did what he wanted, though he listened to others patiently. He was quiet in the presense of Abba Mian. Zamir still recalled one incident from those days. It was early morning and visitors had gathered in the drawing room. Abba Mian's voice was trembling with rage and his face had turned red. It was unusual for the people to congregate so early in the morning. Abba Mian never opened the drawing room that early, nor did any visitors come at that time. The night had been hot and still. Because of the heat, he had spent a restless night and had seen Badi Apa trying to coax the air with a handheld fan. He woke up very early in the morning because of the heat. There was a dust storm and the entire courtyard looked yellow. Dust had covered everything—the terrace, the walls, and the neem tree. Then the storm subsided. Badi Apa sat on her prayer chowki and recited the *Munajat* in her sweet, poignant voice: 'Maula Ali, Wakil Ali, Badshah Ali.'

Every day, after her morning prayers, she recited the *Munajat* and her voice rang like silver-bells in his ears while he was still in bed, half-asleep: 'Maula Ali, Wakil Ali, Badshah Ali…'

Badi Apa's voice had a strange charm and poignancy. It appeared as if her recital of the *Munajat* would soon melt into the sandalwood-coloured dawn. In the still, sweltering, dusty air of the courtyard, Badi Apa's sweet and tender voice paved a cool bright path before him and his eyes began to close. But would the still, oppressive day let him sleep? He sat up. Badi Apa was reciting the *Munajat*, Tai Amma was performing ablutions, Tahsina was sleeping like a log and snoring, and the noise of people talking was coming from the drawing room. He felt bored, got off the cot, and dashed to the drawing room.

'Buniyad Ali, did you hear what Pirji said?' Abba Mian was shouting. 'Arre Pirji, you may contradict me, but what do you have to say about the newspaper report? Do you want me to get the newspaper and show it to you?'

At the mention of the newspaper, Pirji became a little nervous, but Buniyad Ali was impressed by Abba Mian.

Abba Mian spoke even louder, 'This is not all. Listen.' Abba Mian paused and raised his voice to address Pirji: 'Pirji, listen to this! The dome of Huzoor Prophet's tomb has also been razed to the ground.'

'The dome has been razed?' Buniyad Ali, Maulvi Sanaullah, Sheikh Ziaul Haq, all shuddered.

'No, Sahib, this is unimaginable.'

'No, Sahib?' Abba Mian thundered, 'Then surely these newspapers lie.'

That silenced everyone.

Pirji said, 'It has not been razed. It has only been dismantled and kept aside.'

Abba Mian answered, 'Then how come this afternoon, while the rest of Madina was dry, a cloud floated over the holy tomb, rained, and cleansed the holy dome and courtyard of all the dirt?'

All bowed their heads low with reverence. Pirji was silent. Tears rolled down the cheeks of Maulvi Sanaullah. Baba sat quietly in a corner on a stool. He had come home on leave yesterday. Though present, he neither supported any argument nor opposed it; his face betrayed no sign of any emotion, anger, or reverence. To each his own. Baba was just the opposite of Abba Mian.

Abba Mian continued to smoke his huqqa and then passed it to Buniyad Ali. 'Sheikhji, you judge.'

He again said, 'Does such a man deserve to be called a Musalman?'

'Such a man cannot be a Musalman.'

'No, never.'

'And can a man supporting such a man be a Musalman?'

'Never.'

'Then, listen!' Abba Mian said, 'Your Hazrat Raisul Ahrar supported Ibn-Saud.'

'Supported Ibn-Saud?'

'Yes, by God, he supported Ibn-Saud. Let the liar be a heretic. The newspaper is here. His speech is cited in it.'

Pirji again protested, 'Raisul Ahrar's plea was…'

Now it was Maulvi Sanaullah's turn to speak, 'This is about religion. How does this influence his political position?'

'There you go, Sahib,' Abba Mian laughed sarcastically and turned to Buniyad Ali, 'Buniyad Ali, do you hear what Sheikhji says…Arre Sheikhji, you are a Congressman. I am referring to a handful of Musalmans.'

Buniyad Ali passed the huqqa to Abba Mian once again. Abba Mian pressed the nozzle of the pipe between his lips and took a few puffs. He began to cough; a few more puffs and his eyes slowly began to close.

'Anyway, he will pay for his actions. Now, he is no more. May Allah forgive his sins!' Buniyad Ali sighed.

Abba Mian's eyes remained closed and the huqqa continued to gurgle.

'By the way, is this news correct?' Maulvi Sanaullah asked sceptically.

'Sahib, I've heard, Allah knows the truth!' Buniyad Ali answered.

'The newspapers have not reported it yet. What can one say?' Pirji said.

Abba Mian coughed, put aside the huqqa pipe, and said, 'If it is in today's news, the newspaper will reach us tomorrow.'

He again took the pipe of the huqqa in his mouth and closed his eyes.

'I hope it's untrue,' Sheikh Ziaul Haq said. Outside, on the road, a subtle chaos began to build up and they heard the shuffle of several footsteps.

'Why, Bhai, what procession is this?' A passer-by stopped on the road and asked.

'A procession!' Everyone sitting in the drawing room was startled.

The procession reached the path in front of the house.

A large mob of khaddar-clad Congress volunteers and elite Muslims in Turkish fez and sherwanis was walking behind a black flag. Sheikh Ziaul Haq, Pirji, Buniyad Ali, Maulvi Sanaullah, all came out to the front veranda of the house, and then walked down the stairs to join the procession.

Abba Mian also quietly got up and went to the front veranda. Baba was behind him. When the procession marched past the house, Abba Mian too, perhaps unwillingly, slowly climbed down the stairs and became a part of the procession.

Grocer Faqir Chand stepped out of his shop. 'Mian, what has happened?'

'Maulana Mohammad Ali…'

'Mohammad Ali and Shaukat Ali?'

'Yes, Mohammad Ali and Shaukat Ali. Lalaji, shut the shop quickly.'

'Lalaji, what's happened, some bad news?'

'Yes, Mohammad Ali and Shaukat Ali passed away.' Faqir Chand locked his shop and ran to join the procession.

'Mohammad Ali and Shaukat Ali of the Khilafat Movement?'

'Why, what happened? Has the Mohammad Ali of Khilafat Movement passed away?'

Shops began to pull their shutters down. Some chose to lock their shops and sit outside to express grief, while others joined the procession. The silent procession passed through the streets and lanes before reaching the thatheri lane. From there, the procession proceeded to the Bada Bazaar and then congregated in the open field.

'Friends, sit down,' a man said in a loud voice, and the crowd silently sat down on the carpeted ground. Then Samad moved forward and climbed onto the stage covered with white sheets. Wearing a loose khaddar kurta, bespectacled, with long hair, Samad always led all the Congress processions. Sometimes, he would disappear for months and would not be seen in any procession. We would learn that he was in jail. Suddenly, he would reappear, leading a march with a flag in his hands, loudly shouting slogans and delivering full-throated speeches. Today he had not shouted any slogans. He stood on the stage. The crowd was silent. He stood silently for a few moments and then said in a loud voice, 'Brothers, fellow countrymen, today Raisul Ahrar...' His voice broke, he couldn't speak any more. The crowd too was silent. Many people stared at him, others hung their heads low. Some people began to sob silently. A man passed a glass of water to Samad. Samad drank it, wiped his face with his handkerchief, cleared his throat, and spoke confidently, 'My fellow countrymen, Raisul Ahrar had declared that he will not come back to his country till it attains complete independence.' Samad fell silent. And, then, sorrowfully, he exclaimed, 'So, Muslims! Raisul Ahrar did not come back... He has...he has left us.' Samad's voice choked and he got down from the stage. The crowd sat motionless. Silent. Heads hung low. Tears flowed down from a few eyes. Zamir looked at Abba Mian. Tears were streaming down Abba Mian's eyes. Baba watched in silence.

Two

Now, the past floated around him like a fragrance; like an interminable sequence of long nights and scorching afternoons; like a half-forgotten dream. Everything was the same as before and yet not the same—the neem tree in the courtyard, the broad and wide roofs, the rusted railings and high walls, the parapet on the highest terrace which the monkeys had half broken, the red temple at some distance, and, beyond the red temple, neem, peepal, teak trees, and the large factory. How distant they seemed to him, as though he had met them in another life. He had come back after years. He may never have come back. But when the telegram about Abba Mian's illness arrived, Baba quickly picked up his walking stick, Ammi packed for the journey, and they set out. But it was not a journey of a few hours; it was a journey of days. After all, one can't travel from one state to another in an instant! The train moved the whole day, the whole night, halted, moved again. It halted at some station in the darkness of the night or in some jungle. It blew its whistle. At times, it halted for so long that groups of passengers, tired and annoyed, jumped down and walked on the gravel spread between the railway tracks. Baba, too, fidgeted in his seat, looked out of the window, and finally got off the train to make enquiries with the ticket collector. Far in the distance, a big round disc of light appeared, and a train came thundering down the tracks with an ear-splitting sound; brightly lit coaches full of passengers swiftly passed by the stationary train, and then disappeared into the darkness, leaving behind a slowly fading trail of sound. After a while, our stationary train jolted into motion, the coaches shuddered, and the train started moving again.

Many times during the journey, Ammi worried about her twitching left eye. Early morning, on the third day, she noticed a dead bull lying on the dirt-road ahead of the running train. Instinctively, she exclaimed, 'May Allah have mercy!' The train stopped. The rest of her journey was spent in anxiety.

Baba had left in a hurry, but Abba Mian was in a greater hurry. When we reached, Teeja was over. Badi Apa hugged Baba and wept profusely; wailed; and as she wailed, she chided him for not having arrived in time to offer water to his dying father; she complained; cast aspersions; spoke about how Abba Mian had waited for him and her own nervousness, all by turn.

'Till his last breath, his eyes remained fixed on the door hoping that you would come. 'Chhammo,' he would ask again and again, 'have you sent someone to the railway station?' He was desperate to see his son.' Badi Apa's voice became tearful again, and tears filled Baba's eyes. They had arrived just before dawn. It was still dark. Who knew how long Badi Apa had clung to Baba and Amma and wept, for Zamir had dozed off as soon as he lay down on the string cot. When he woke up in the morning, he saw that they were still lamenting. Badi Apa was, however, calmer, and in between sobs, she paused, chopped beetle-nuts with a sarautta, and talked. Though, whenever she suddenly recalled something related to Abba Mian, tears welled up in her eyes, her voice became husky, and she would start weeping loudly. Baba sat quietly with his head bowed and his eyes full of tears. Every now and then, he would take a handkerchief out of his pocket and cover his eyes. His eyes were red, though not as swollen as Badi Apa's. He was sad that he had not seen Abba Mian before his death or helped him, and was disturbed by Badi Apa's wailing and taunting.

'Bibi! Except for his desire to have his son shoulder his dead body—may Allah rest his soul in peace—Allah answered all his other wishes.' In the midst of the grief, Tai Amma's voice carried a touch of comfort. 'May Allah grant death only after one's children are well settled! May Allah bring such a peaceful death to everyone.' Suddenly, Tai Amma remembered something and fell silent. She stared into empty space. She sat quietly for a while and, then, as if startled by something, said, 'Bibi, he seemed to be sleeping—as if he had just gone off to sleep and would wake up at the slightest sound.'

Badi Apa stared at Badi Amma's face. Then she began to relate something else, 'He asked me what day of the week it was. I said, Thursday. Tahsina was sitting near his feet. He stared at her. Then, he asked me to recite the *Naad-i-Ali*.

I began to recite the *Naad-i-Ali*...suddenly, he opened his eyes wide and stared at the door...as though someone was standing there...He said: Chhammo, Maula has come... and then he slowly shut his eyes.'

Everyone sat quietly without moving, lost in their own thoughts. Zamir looked at Badi Apa, whose voice, for once, had not faltered.

'Maula Mushkil Kusha visits us at the moment of death.' Tai Amma's pensive voice emerged softly like a whisper and receded. The same stillness engulfed everything once again. The courtyard was at peace. Even the sunlight had stopped at the lower end of the string-cot. Small white neem flowers fell softly and gently from the branches above on someone's lap, or shoulder, or head—lay scattered on Badi Apa's head resting on her knees, Tai Amma's snow-white hair and Ammi's greying hair, the paandan, the string-cot, and the new, ochre-coloured surahis resting on a stand.

Somehow, the conversation that carried out in whispers turned once again to the same subject. Tai Amma's voice was so low that it was barely audible. One could only see her lips move and her big eyes open with surprise. Badi Apa stopped chopping betel nuts with mechanical regularity . . .

'Badi Apa, my heart sank,' Ammi's voice was a little louder than whisper now. 'I told your brother, but he snubbed me. My faith was weak, he said. There are villages all around. Some farmer's bull must have died. But, Apa, my heart throbbed uncontrollably. Allah, why should the train have stopped in the middle of the jungle? There was no field or village close by; whose bull could it have been?'

'Arre, Bahannu,' Badi Apa's voice was now louder than a whisper and her eyes were full of surprise. 'Bahannu, I had dreamt of it, three days earlier. I heard Abba Mian call out in my dream: Chhammo, Chhammo! I came out to the veranda. His back was towards me and he was walking towards the door. I asked: Abba Mian, where are you going when hot and dusty winds are blowing? He replied: Bibi, the winds are not hot; the day is ending; soon there'll be a call for prayer and I am going to read the namaz. Lock the door from the inside.'

Everyone sat still like statues . . . silent . . . lost in some distant thought. The branches of the neem tree, swaying in the wind a while ago, were now still and drooping and little white flowers floated slowly in the wind like spiders' webs before reaching the ground.

Restless, Tai Amma said, 'God forbid, it's so hot. The wind is still.' And she began to quickly move her handheld fan.

Badi Apa jumped up. She remembered that Baba had to bathe. 'Tahsina, ari Tahsina! Bibi go, place a towel and soap in the bathroom, and see if there's enough water in the tub.'

Every now and then, as she talked, Badi Apa would remember Abba Mian and tears would well up in her eyes. At first, this happened frequently, then after longer and longer intervals. The mood of sorrow began to lift from the haveli and concerns of daily life took over. Memories of Abba Mian began to recede and Baba became the centre of Badi Apa's attention. Besides, Ammi too had come to visit after many years; hundreds of things, important and not-so-important, had to be shared with her. And, when Badi Apa noticed Zamir, she wondered when he would get married.

'Mashallah, he has finished his education and is so grown-up! Look, Bahu, marry him off now!'

Ammi replied, 'Badi Apa, your brother says that we should not force him to get married against his wishes. He belongs to the new generation and their choice is not the same as that of their parents. In fact, your brother says we should let him find his own bride. We'll only perform the wedding rituals.'

'Why, Zamir beta! What kind of bride do you want?' Badi Apa turned to him.

Tai Amma joined in, 'Aji, he'll not tell you, he'll tell me. Beta, come and whisper in my ears. I'll find the one you want!'

'Yes, why not, brides are like cucumbers and vegetables, you go to the market and buy them!' Badi Apa snapped, 'Tai Amma, good brides can't be found on the roadside!'

But, before he realised it, the conversation subtly drifted away to something else. Instead of talking about his marriage, they began to discuss the affairs of girls and boys in general, and the conversation took an entirely new direction.

He was once again engrossed in reading *Alif Laila*. He had chosen to sit in a place where the sun reached late. It was under the dense neem tree, a little away from the rows of tulsi and bela. There was a concrete platform for the earthen pitchers which was built against the wall near the neem tree. New earthen pitchers with garlands of flowers encircling their long necks and brightly polished Muradabadi drinking glasses were placed on the cement platform. White neem flowers were scattered everywhere—on the ground, over the wet plates covering the clay pitchers, in the paan tray nearby, and the drinking glasses. He had placed his wicker stool between the flower bed and the stand for the clay pitchers against the wall, and claimed it as his permanent seat. Badi Apa, Ammi, and Tai Amma sat on a string-cot and gossiped, chopping betel nuts as they opened and shut the lid of the paandan with a clank. Sometimes, when Baba felt suffocated in the drawing room, he came and sat on a cot under the neem tree. Yellow, brittle, and faded papers lay scattered on the ground, as Baba read them carefully and arranged them safely in a file. In spite of his diligence, he had not found a single document which could help us win the court case and recover the haveli. Tall, thin like a stick, with greying hair and a wheatish complexion, he was the first in his family to be employed by the government and to wear trousers. Tai Amma had always objected to his ways, 'Aji, he had the same habits even before he became a tahsildar. He always wore breeches and clipped-clopped around in boots, and when he came back from hunting, he'd drop his gun in a corner, throw down the bag on his shoulder, chuck his full-boots on one side, and offer namaz. I'd yell: Shibbu Mian, at least change out of your breeches before performing the wazu! But would Shibbu Mian ever listen? Tai Amma, he would retort that people perform namaz even in England where nobody wears pyjamas. To hell with the English, I would shout, if people begin to offer namaz in breeches and trousers then doomsday isn't far away. And, Bibi, after he became a tahsildar, he acquired all the other habits of a gentleman. Abba Mian used to taunt me: Tai Amma, your Bashir Hussain has become a complete Englishman. You raised him, now take care of him! Ai Mian, how could I? I raised him, but didn't expect him to become an Englishman! With age, however, he slowly gave up his English habits.' As for his job as a tahsildar, initially, he came here whenever he could get leave. But after Abba Mian passed away, his responsibilities increased. He thought that since he was close to retirement and had rarely taken leave, he should stay back at home. Besides the lawsuit for the haveli, there were lands to be looked after and farms to be managed. He also wanted to build a kothi with his retirement funds. He woke up early, went to inspect his farms, surveyed the ground where he wanted to build his kothi and, after he came back, he sat hunched over those faded, yellow papers. When he got tired of reading them, he took off his spectacles and placed them on those papers. Though a man of few words, he couldn't help making a few suggestions once in a while. And Badi Apa, who paid attention to her brother's remarks, was always quick to retort: That would be a disaster!

Baba responded dryly, 'Abba Mian has already done enough damage. Where would the money to repay such heavy loans come from?'

Grief-stricken and with tears in her eyes, Badi Apa replied, 'The lands are already lost, now the last memory of our ancestors…' Badi Apa couldn't continue. After a while she added, 'Amma ji departed from this haveli. Abba Mian opened his eyes in this house and died here too. This is where Bade Abba too breathed his last.' Tears streamed down Badi Apa's cheeks and Baba turned to read the papers once again, desultorily at first and then with attention.

The haveli, which to Zamir was like a continent, rose before his eyes: its spacious rooms with high-beamed roofs, wide verandas with arches and pillars, dark, dusty storerooms which he was always frightened to peep into, lest the resident scorpion of the storeroom enticed him in, basements which were so vast that he had no clue where they began and where they ended, an iron-barred window under the raised veranda which overlooked the courtyard and another window that opened into the room adjacent to the veranda, and yet another window attached to the dingy anteroom of the big hall. The haveli had long and wide terraces which merged with staircases like rail tracks at a junction, and which felt like alien lands the moment one stepped on to them. Grass grew on the clay-baked terraces during the rains, but once the rains stopped, the grass withered into small, sharp stubble and looked like remains from an ancient past. The dry, scum-encrusted, narrow drains on the terrace looked like parched streams. Then there was that haunted blackened boundary wall of the haveli which was covered with white bird droppings.

On the other side of the boundary wall, spread far into the distance, lay countless roofs of different heights. And beyond them was the Lal Mandir, a tall building made of red stone, which seemed like yet another continent. Except for the Lal Mandir, the haveli was the tallest building in the basti. Its expanse and height could be fully appreciated when Tai Amma talked about the mutiny. 'Bibi, I wasn't even born then. Badi Amma used to tell us that there was so much destruction and confusion that year that no one knew what had happened to the others in our neighbourhood. Thriving bastis were completely ruined. For miles, there was no one left to light a fire in the hearth or burn a lamp in the evening.

Jats, Gujjars, and Angathpurbis carrying their lances and spears, ran from one end to the other, looting this village today, attacking that basti the next day, and ransacking another town the following day. Not a single town or village was spared. At such a time, everyone here got together, sent their wives to the haveli, and began to guard the basti with their lathis. Since the haveli's roof was the tallest, anyone approaching the basti could be spotted from a distance. Three men kept watch from the terrace with a drum. They kept a vigil day and night. The damned Gujjars attacked our basti thrice, but each time the warning beat of the drums forced them to retreat.'

The height and the expanse of the haveli was still the same. But how old it now seemed! Some domes and arches were ruined beyond repair. The rest were also in a bad shape. The boundary wall had turned black and its plaster had peeled off in huge chunks. The bare bricks were now visible and the yellow clay, used to hold them together, had turned into powder. In the veranda, inside the rooms, on the floors, in the corners, everywhere there were heaps of yellow dust crawling with insects and bugs of all kinds. What did not look ancient was the vast expansive courtyard daubed with clay. When the waterman first sprinkled water on it, steam rose from the ground, but soon after, the clay dried again. It was only after many buckets of water had been sprinkled that the ground could retain its moisture. Baba was tempted to step outside when the scent of wet clay mingled with that of the freshly lit huqqa kept next to his stool. No one knew how long the neem tree, which was still as dense and green as ever and gave shade to everyone, had been standing in the courtyard. Baba had watched it since he was a child. The ground near the platform for the surahis looked like a bed of sweet-smelling flowers; it was always moist because water perpetually seeped from the clay pots. Graceful, fair hands with long fingers poured out water with a soft gurgling sound from a long-necked surahi.

After drinking water, Tahsina left the glass behind the pitcher and walked back to the kitchen without paying him any attention. He turned to *Alif Laila* again, a book he had pulled out from Abba Mian's library and was reading to pass the time. However, he soon got so engrossed in it that he began to live in the world of beautiful temptresses and their palaces . . . 'There is no breeze!' When Badi Apa's voice startled him out of his reverie and dragged him out of *Alif Laila's* palace, he realised that his body was drenched in sweat. He saw a green and red-striped fan moving in Badi Apa's hands. 'If there is such a swarm of flies now, what would happen in the rainy season?' Tai Amma sighed, 'Bibi, if only it would rain! Ashadh is nearly over and not a drop of rain has fallen so far. Tauba, it's so hot this year. My legs are covered with prickly heat.'

Then the neem leaves stirred a little and Ammi exclaimed, 'Thank God!' Suddenly, a dove began to coo and Bunni mimicked its sound. The dove stopped, fluttered its wings, rose to the sky, swept down, and flew past the rooftop.

Tahsina came out of the kitchen and sat next to the bed of tulsi plants. As she plucked some tulsi leaves, she moved up close to the stool on which he was sitting. He noticed drops of sweat trickle down her long, elegant neck and a few strands of hair, which had escaped from her braids, cling to it; her transparent viol kurta was damp and stuck to her shapely fair back. He quickly turned his gaze away and buried himself in the pages of *Alif Laila* once again; but within seconds, his glance inevitably wandered back to her plaited hair, her lovely neck, and her attractive back, as her long and elegant fingers plucked green mint leaves.

One day, full of sympathy, Ammi blurted out, 'Badi Apa, this work is taxing, it'll drain the life out of poor Tahsina; single-handedly, she takes care of the haveli. It's not fair!'

Badi Apa replied, 'What is so taxing about it? If she'll not do the work, will someone from outside do it?'

'Badi Apa,' Ammi answered, 'you are really cruel to leave all the work to her.'

'Aji, unmarried girls should get used to doing household chores. After all, they'll go to somebody else's house after they are married. Who'll feed them there if they don't work?'

'Ai lo, Badi Apa, your reasoning is topsy-turvy! In fact, the only time girls can enjoy life is at their parents' house. Once married, will they have this luxury? No, Bibi, it's not fair. Besides, how long will I sit idle...'

'No, Bahu, I'll not let you go into the kitchen,' Badi Apa at once protested.

Ammi gave up. Tahsina continued to do all the work. The routine of the house resumed. Tahsina's frugality brought about one change, though. Ammi began to leave money in her safekeeping. Therefore, Zamir had to stretch his hand before Tahsina every day. 'How much?' she would ask. Though she gave what he asked, she always urged him not to waste it. Achhe and Bunni would appear from somewhere and fleece him of every single anna, and then would triumphantly go around the house announcing it. Badi Apa would snub Bunni, and then scold Zamir, 'Beta, why do you give her money? A glutton that she is, she will rush to the market and squander it all there.' Tai Amma would bless him profusely for giving money to Achhe, 'May he become an officer like his father, may he rule, may he get married, may he get a moonlike bride, may his parents see him blossom!' Tai Amma's hair had turned grey, but her body was still in good shape. Her pyjamas were still tight around her legs and, in spite of wrinkles on her face, it was clear that she must have been beautiful once. On the other hand, there was Badi Apa. She seemed to have shrunk physically; her well-built body was now only skin and bones; her clothes sagged. He still did not know why she was called Tai Amma by everyone in the house. How was Tai Amma related to him or to others? Even Abba Mian called her Tai Amma. All he remembered of her daughter was that she was a big-eyed, tall, and fair woman. After the wedding of Tai Amma's daughter, Badi Apa had commented, 'The girl is ruined. These people are uncouth rustics.' And Ammi had taunted, 'Now a star is not going to come down and marry her. He is good enough. These people are poor, but they will keep the girl happy.' When and how all that happened, he could not recall. What he did remember was the day news of her death arrived; and when Tai Amma returned after the forty days of mourning, she had a chubby, fair baby with her whom she began to call Achhe.

Achhe and Bunni would dart out like arrows as soon as they got the money and would come back sucking green, red, or orange-coloured ice.

When he got tired of sitting on the stool, he would stop reading *Alif Laila*, yawn, and then close his eyes. In the meantime, Badi Apa would call out from the hall, 'Arre Bhai, where is Zamir? Is he still sitting outside? Tahsina, serve Bhaiyya food.' Tahsina would come out and order him curtly, 'Come and eat your food!' And he would quietly get up and go inside. There were times when he was so depressed that he did not feel like eating. He would be angry at himself, at Tahsina, at the still wind, at the swarm of flies, and at the unending holidays. Tahsina would then return and order him in the same abrupt, impersonal tone, 'Come and eat your food.' He would quietly put his book aside and follow her.

Three

'Mango stone, o mango stone, where will I go after I am married?' The soft raw mango stone slipped out of Bunni's delicate fingers and fell off the cot.

There was a mound of green mango peels and clean mango stones on one side of the cot. Next to it was a large tray, piled high with freshly peeled raw mangoes. Tahsina was chopping raw mangoes, removing their stones with the edge of a knife, and placing slices of mangoes on the tray.

Bunni picked up a clean, white mango stone, stood near the stool on which Zamir was sitting, and asked, 'Zamir Bhai, tell me, where will I go after I am married?'

'You make a guess.' He was so engrossed in reading *Alif Laila* that he didn't want to be distracted.

Bunni asked the mango stone first about her marriage, then about Achhe's and Zamir Bhai's marriage. 'Zamir Bhai, you will marry someone from the West.'

'Really?' he answered indifferently and continued to read his book.

'Mango stone, O mango stone, whom will Baji marry?'

The stone fell on Zamir's open book.

Bunni clapped and shouted, 'Aha-ha-ha, Baji will marry Zamir Bhai.'

His heart sank, the blood in his veins dried up, and his hands and feet froze. All he wanted was to somehow leave, disappear from there. But he could not move; his gaze was fixed on his book and his heart pounded madly. The air was oppressive and the neem leaves drooped in silence. His neck and hands were covered with sweat which dripped down his collar. And then a thin line of perspiration trickled down his back and soaked his shirt. He wanted to shut the book and sneak out of the house quietly, but his body refused to budge. He didn't dare look at Tahsina, but the soft sound of the knife cutting through the raw mangoes and edging out the stones continued as steadily as before without faltering. There still was no breeze and the neem leaves continued to hang in silence. A dove flew up to the branch of the neem tree and began to coo. Bunni's attention shifted from the mango stone to the dove and she began to mimic it.

'Have you memorised this morning's lesson?' Tahsina asked, interrupting Munni's mimicry.

'Le-ss-o-n.'

'Yes, lesson.' Tahsina repeated in the same composed voice and, picking up her knife and the tray, got up from the cot.

Bunni was quiet.

'Sit down and read your *Siparah* book,' Tahsina admonished her sharply.

Bunni froze with fear. Suddenly a prisoner, all her pertness disappeared. Helpless, she slowly picked up her *Siparah* book and took it out of its cloth case. Her hands, which a while ago seemed full of energy while asking the mango stone about her marriage, lost their verve and were forced to obey orders. Half-heartedly, she opened her *Siparah* book, turned its pages, and began to read.

Tahsina lifted the tray full of raw mangoes, walked to the cot placed in the sun, emptied the tray on it, and began to spread raw mangoes over it.

Zamir quietly closed his book, placed it on the stool, and crept away.

The silence in the lane outside seemed to buzz as if bees had swarmed out of a hive which had been smashed. Parts of the lane, which ran next to a few tall houses, were shaded. A dog, panting with its tongue hanging out, was sitting in a pool of muddy drain water. At the sound of footsteps, it crawled out of the puddle, shook its wet body, and sprayed drops of dirty water in every direction. As Zamir walked out of the lane into the next one, a flock of drowsy hens raised their heads in alarm and cackled loudly. For a moment, Zamir felt as though he had entered the zenana of a stranger's house and that many eyes were fixed on him. He continued to walk slowly. He had barely taken a few steps when a rooster fluttered it wings and crowed behind him. Another spotless white rooster, sitting on the boundary wall ahead, was so startled that it cocked its head, flapped its wings rapidly, and crowed loudly.

He walked through the lane to the Lal Mandir Square. In the heat, its red stones were burning hot. The stone platform around the well too was scorching. The iron pulleys fixed on the edge of the dry well were silent.

A shiver run through his body as he walked through the water-tank lane. But, within a few seconds, he was in the thatheri wali gali which was full of sunlight and dust. The sound of hammers falling on shapeless metal to make large plates, pots, and trays of brass and copper was so loud that every other sound was drowned. Gradually that clanging sound too faded, lost in the path disappearing behind him. A black bull stood stubbornly in the middle of the kunjdon wali gali. When it refused to budge even after being cajoled, he quietly crept out of the lane by keeping close to the wall so as to avoid its horns and hoofs. From there, he walked through the qasai mohalla, and then skipped across the metalled road to the barren land, and from the barren land walked down the road to the cultivated fields.

Gandal got up when he saw him. 'Abe, Hira,' he called out, 'Chhote Mian has come. Bring a cot.'

Hira came running with a cot, put it down for Zamir, and asked, 'Mian ji, should I get something to eat or drink?'

'No, Bhai.'

Gandal sat down beside the cot with his chillum. No one was eager to draw water from the well at that time. Gandal and Hira were totally at peace. Gandal placed the pipe of his chillum in his mouth and shut his eyes. Hira was excited by Zamir's visit. His eyes sparkled and he was eager to ask him something but could not.

'Chhote Mian,' he said, at last finding his voice, 'they say a kothi will be built here. Will the entire haveli be shifted to this place? When Abba Mian was alive, this place was very lively. During the harvest season, everyone used to gather here. But after him…' Hira's voice faltered, 'only Ram Naam.'

He could not say anything more. Gandal too was silent. His eyes were shut as he continued to puff on his huqqa.

Hira spoke again, 'Chhote Mian, I hope that the tahsildar sahib will stay this time?'

'Abey, of course,' Gandal replied on Zamir's behalf. 'Once he gets his pension, he'll stay.'

'So, Chhote Mian, will you also stay?'

'Lalla has yet to finish his studies,' Gandal once again replied on Zamir's behalf, as he opened his eyes, coughed, passed the chillum to Hira, and said, 'Chhote Mian, centuries have passed! When will your studies end?'

'Soon,' he replied.

But Gandal was not listening to him. His gaze had shifted away to watch the play of light and shade over the green fields; a wave of sunlight swiftly swept over them, followed immediately by shadows. A thin layer of clouds slowly spread over the fields as the sunlight skipped away, caressing the rows of trees beyond the fields. He too looked up, as Gandal and Hira turned their gaze to the sky. A few patches of clouds floating in the sky had overshadowed the sun.

'Gandal,' Hira whispered softly, 'what does the sky indicate? I no longer have the strength to pull water out of the well. If it doesn't rain soon, my arms will give way.' He slowly passed the chillum to Gandal.

Gandal quietly puffed at his chillum and meditatively replied, 'This time the rains will be delayed. Jyotishiji was saying that the year will be tough.' He took another puff and passed the chillum back to Hira, 'Lala, it needs to be relit. Add another upla to it.'

Hira took the huqqa and crouched near the storeroom where the uplas were kept.

Gandal's eyes again began to close and he hummed softly:

You wasted your nights in sleep, your days in eating.
Hira, your life was priceless; you exchanged it for nothing.

Gandal's eyes were closed; his body was motionless, as if all the energy had drained out of it with his words and slowly dissipated.

Zamir quietly got up from the cot and walked back home. Sunlight once again swept over the trees beyond the fields, spread over the fields, and the entire garrison of shadows departed.

By the time he reached home, the sun had begun to set. Evening shadows had covered the courtyard in front of the porch; the doors of the hall were still shut and the bamboo curtain covering the veranda was still damp. From the courtyard, he walked up to the portico towards the hall when his steps faltered and he turned to the room next to the hall.

His entrance startled Ammi and Tai Amma, who were in the middle of a gossip session.

'Ai hai, where were you all afternoon?' Ammi immediately asked.

'I just went to the farm for a while.'

'To the farm? Are you crazy, boy? Hot and dusty winds are blowing and this prince has been roaming in the fields.'

'Oh, just look at his face. It's red,' Tai Amma added irritably.

'Come, my son, lie down for a while. Let me cool you down with a pankha.'

The suggestion offered him a reprieve, and he immediately took off his shoes and shirt and lay down.

Tai Amma began to move the pankha vigorously. His eyes began to close.

Everybody rested in the hall because Noory pulled a large pankha with frills which hung from the ceiling all through the afternoon, and the khas curtains on the doors were kept moist till the evening. Ammi now often came from the hall to the next room on the pretext that the children were making too much noise. Tai Amma too joined her and, instead of sleeping, they chatted, sometimes in whispers and sometimes loudly.

'Aji, there is one thing,' Tai Amma was saying, 'this cursed girl is quite spoilt. She wanders all day. Is this how one studies? To study, you need concentration. After all, I am only human and sometimes lose my temper at her.'

'Tai Amma, how can you say that!' Ammi retorted. 'All children are mischievous. Is your Achhe any less naughty?'

'Ai, he is the naughtiest. He makes me shout so much that my head begins to spin.'

'That's it, Tai Amma. Children are naughty, but you don't kill them for it. But when Tahsina thrashed her sister with one end of her fan, my heart just sank.'

'Yes, of course. I don't understand why people can't treat others like human beings?' Tai Amma said, and then fell silent.

In a hushed voice, Ammi added, 'Tai Amma, Tahsina's a little crazy. When she works, she works relentlessly; when she sits down to teach her little sister, it's as if the child must learn everything in a day.'

'Oh, that's a genetic trait,' Tai Amma said, 'Is her mother any different? Once she gets an idea, that's it. And your husband? Now, Mashallah, he has children, responsibilities… you should have seen him when he was a child. He was so stubborn that even if Abba Mian got angry, he would not give in.'

'Yes, indeed it's a genetic trait, but Tai Amma, this is different.' Ammi's voice became even more hushed and she began to whisper, 'Aji, how long will Chhammo Apa keep her unmarried? Mashallah, she has come of age. Apa should now worry about getting her married.'

'Yes, Bibi! She has, of course, come of age. She's only a bit older than your Zamir.'

'Aji, Tai Amma, Tahsina is a lot older than Zamir.'

'No, Bibi!' Tai Amma corrected her firmly. 'When she was born, you were pregnant, expecting Zamir. I vividly remember it as if it happened today. When Chhammo took her chhalla bath, all the ladies said, lo Bibi, now that Shibbu Mian's sister is safe, may God help his wife deliver her child safely. You were seven months pregnant then.'

'Anyway, even a couple of months' difference is a lot. Girls grow faster. Don't you see, she looks twice Zamir's age?'

'Yes, Mashallah, she's a nice-looking girl.'

'What's Badi Apa waiting for?'

'Who knows what she's waiting for! It's not as though there are no proposals! Her chacha's son is ready to marry

Tahsina. To be honest, do chachas or tayas care after a girl's father is dead? But that damn fellow longs for his niece.'

'What does the fellow do?' asked Ammi.

'Who knows what he does! He's uneducated and no good. When Buniyad Ali visited in the month of Madar, I asked, Aji, Buniyad Ali, when will your Imdad pass his entrance exam? He said, Tai Amma, what's the use of passing entrance exams when even a BA pass loiters around unemployed? Nobody cares for degrees. I've decided that Imdad will join the police force. In two years, he may even become an inspector. Yes, Bibi, once he's an inspector, what more could he want? He'll be like a lord. What'll he do with a useless degree? Lick it?'

'Aji, Tai Amma, do you think one becomes an inspector just like that, for free? When BAs can't become one, how can that lout?'

'Bibi, how would I know about your goddamned thanedari and tehsildari? I only know what Buniyad Ali said.'

'Buniyad Ali Chacha's words mean nothing; he just brags. But what do I care? If Imdad becomes a thanedar, would I be unhappy, especially if a daughter of our family marries him? I think, Badi Apa shouldn't hesitate any more. The fellow is not that bad either. Now, a star is not going to descend from the heavens for Tahsina.'

'Who can read her mind? Who knows what she's thinking?' Tai Amma said meaningfully. 'When Abba Mian was alive, every time the topic came up for discussion, he became silent. No one knew what he wanted!'

There was a sudden gush of wind and the door of the room opened and shut with a bang.

'There's a storm coming,' Tai Amma exclaimed.

Zamir too opened his eyes with a start. A pale yellow light engulfed the veranda and the courtyard.

'Everyone, pick up your clothes drying outside; the wind is very strong,' Badi Apa shouted from the courtyard.

Tai Amma and Ammi ran out of the room to gather the clothes hanging on the lines and the mattresses spread on the cots outside.

'Achhe, O Achhe, come inside!' Tai Amma rushed towards the veranda holding Achhe's hand, and then she called out, 'Bibi, come inside, this looks like a violent storm.'

It was a dust storm. All of a sudden, the wind dropped and the fan in Badi Apa's hand began to spin faster; the dove stopped cooing and with a gentle flutter of wings rose from the neem tree, floated in the wind, and then slowly vanished from sight. The sweet, sensuous, and hypnotic song of a cuckoo rose from the dense leaves of the mango tree. The cuckoo's song was cool like the eastern breeze on a hot and sultry day. But soon, the cuckoo stopped singing. Tai Amma grabbed a pankha from Badi Apa, 'Bibi, it's miserably hot; the air is very still.' And Badi Apa unexpectedly turned to Zamir, 'Why are you sitting here? Go and lie down in the hall under the fan. Reading day in and day out is a curse.' Soon, Tai Amma slowly stopped fanning herself. She turned her gaze towards the sky and said, as if talking to herself in a voice in which hope was tinged with doubt, 'Another storm is coming.' All eyes were raised towards the sky, which appeared yellow and, as it darkened, countless kites, slowly wheeling in circles, flew round and round in ecstasy. Suddenly, an unearthly shiver ran through the neem leaves and a crow, hiding in its thick branches, fluttered out with a start and, shrieking, screeching, and cawing, hurried away to join others in the sky. The cry of birds startled the hens. Alert and tense with apprehension, they raised their necks and cocked their heads to one side as if trying hard to catch a sound. Their nervousness affected everyone in the house too. A window was opened on the second or the third floor and then shut with a loud bang. 'Mian, a storm is coming,' people called out from one terrace to the next. Bedcovers, white sheets, blue saris, and half-dry violet, pink, and turquoise dupattas still hanging from clothes lines in the sun were covered with dust. Elderly women and young girls quickly gathered them and, carrying them across the parapets, ran down the staircases. Doors were hurriedly latched from inside. As the dust storm began to blow with ferocity, the entire area was suddenly steeped in a dusty, yellow light.

Storms do not follow a schedule. Sometimes the sky turns a pale yellow before noon, sometimes late in the afternoon, and sometimes in the evening. These are days when there is a dust storm every afternoon. Every day, however, a large number of kites fly in lazy, drowsy, slightly drunken circles under the sun surrounded by a halo of dust. Then, the cycle of stifling days suddenly snaps at night when everyone is asleep; and a passing storm shatters the trance of people sleeping in courtyards, rooftops, and terraces. Even the colour of the stormy sky is never the same—though usually a dusty yellow, there are mornings when it turns a deep grey, and by noon the landscape is drowned in such deep darkness that lanterns have to be lit in shops and houses.

It didn't matter whether the storms came in the afternoon, evening, or the middle of the night. The devastation they caused was always visible the next morning when vegetable-sellers came with baskets and baskets loaded with raw mangoes that had fallen in the storm and sold them at dirt-cheap prices. These storms not only knocked down raw mangoes, but also snapped branches and uprooted trees loaded with them. Raw mangoes were then heaped on cots in the haveli, and the knives in Tai Amma's and Badi Apa's hands moved rapidly to chop them into small chunks.

'Did you hear what happened? Last night's storm picked up a heavy stone that weighed three tons from Shekhu's Taal and smashed it down on Dinur's thatched hut! The poor fellow's roof was shattered!'

Badi Apa was astonished, 'Tai Amma, I don't believe that.' Then she turned to Zamir, for she had complete faith in his knowledge of science, and whenever she came across something which was beyond reason, she turned to him for an answer. 'Zamir Mian, you have read science; tell us, can a three-ton stone fly?'

Tai Amma didn't give Zamir a chance to respond, 'I don't know about your cursed science, but why not wait and ask the old woman who sells vegetables? She'll surely come tomorrow to sell raw mangoes. Oh yes, that cursed crone's sister-in-law's son was carried away by the storm. He hasn't yet been found.'

Badi Apa contradicted her again, 'I don't believe that a big boy like him can fly away in a storm!'

'Bibi, why is it so difficult to believe? This world is a workshop of wonders—my mind fails me when

I think about the dark storm. Only God knows His secrets.'

'Tai Amma,' Bunni intervened, 'you said there are fairies in dark storms!'

'Bunni, I was only repeating what I've heard…King Inder on his throne, djinns in the front, and djinns behind and fairies all around him.'

'Tai Amma,' Bunni said confidentially. 'Should I tell you who carried away that boy? The fairies!'

Badi Apa fumed, 'Just look at her gossiping away. Have you finished studying for the day? Ari, Tahsina, did you give her homework today?'

Bunni was dumbstruck.

'Bunni, come here, recite your lesson to me,' Tahsina's commanding voice rose from the kitchen.

Her thread of thought broken, Tai Amma turned her attention to the raw mangoes again.

'See, these mango seeds have begun to sprout. Soon, the mangoes will ripen.'

'They are already ripe and sour,' Badi Apa retorted. 'But if it rains heavily, they'll ripen.'

The sky remained a dusty yellow as usual, and the mangoes sour. Neither did the rains fall, nor did the mangoes turn juicy. The sun rose daily as usual; sunlight and shadows played their usual games of hide-and-seek in the vast courtyard of the haveli. Soon, it was excruciatingly hot under the sun. Everybody packed up and went back to the big dimly lit hall, where the cloth-fan with frills swung from the ceiling and the damp khas screens on the doors cooled the body and soothed the eyes. First, a dastarkhwan was spread on the floor and then, after the meal, Tai Amma, Badi Apa, and Ammi lay down on the floor and slept. 'Bibi, these kids won't let us take a nap even for a second,' Tai Amma grumbled, as she was startled out of her slumber. Then, Badi Apa scolded Bunni, 'Are you going to sleep or not?' Tai Amma grabbed Achhe's arm and forced him to lie down. Soon, her eyes began to droop. Slowly, everyone lying on the floor dozed off. After a long gap, Badi Apa stopped snoring and asked, 'What's the time, Zamir?' 'Half past two.' Badi Apa's eyes drooped once again. Then Tai Amma opened her eyes and, still drowsy, looked out of the door. 'It's still very sunny.' Drowsiness engulfed her once again. The fan continued to swing at its own steady pace till Noory's hands slackened and sleep overwhelmed her. When the fan stopped moving, Noory woke with a start and began to pull the rope again. Badi Apa got up to look out of the door anxiously, 'Oh no, the sun has reached the outer edge of the terrace. The time for zohr has nearly passed.' She quietly slipped out of the room. Zamir shut his eyes and then opened them at once. He could never sleep like Tai Amma or Badi Apa! The day seemed excruciatingly long; the afternoon stretched on and on. Baba took a brief nap and, then, put on his spectacles and reclined against a bolster to read the newspapers. As Tahsina tossed this way and that, her bangles jingled sweetly. When Ammi opened her eyes, she admonished her, 'Beti, can't you rest a little in the afternoons at least!' 'Mumani ji, the starch I prepared yesterday will go bad.' 'Oh yes, if you have some left, wash this also,' Ammi said, taking off her dupatta without getting up and giving it to Tahsina.

He felt suffocated lying in the dark, stuffy room. He got up quietly and went out. The veranda, though scorching hot, was bubbling with activity. Water dripped from the khas screens and trickled across the floor; Achhe and Bunni, who were splashing around in the water, disappeared from the veranda in no time; in the golden light of the setting sun, Tahsina sat near the door next to the veranda with a tub full of starch, a pile of clean and dirty dupattas, detergent, and small paper packets with powders of different dyes. She scrubbed the dupattas thoroughly, rinsed them, then filled the tub with clean water, prepared the required dyes for the dupattas, squeezed water out of them, and spread them on the clothes line to dry in the sun. She then fetched a pot filled with musk-melon pulp, washed it thoroughly in water to separate the white seeds, placed the seeds in a sieve, and poured water over them till they were white and clean. She then dyed some seeds green and some red and strung them together on a string.

When they heard the sound of something fall in one corner of the veranda, they both turned with a start. Suddenly, Achhe and Bunni walked in and began shouting, 'Teliya raja, teliya raja…Zamir Bhai look, teliya raja!' Really! A beetle, as lustrous as if it had been soaked in black oil, buzzed around, crashed against the wall, fell to the ground, and began to dig a hole through the clay floor. But even before they could react, Achhe's eyes caught sight of a wasp near the door of the veranda. It flew from the veranda into the courtyard, and then rose up in the air till it reached the top of the boundary wall. 'A wasp, Bunni, look, a wasp!' Achhe and Bunni shot out like arrows from the veranda, ran through the courtyard, climbed up the stairway, and disappeared. Once again, Tahsina and he were left alone in the haunting silence of the veranda. He yearned for those moments of privacy, but when they actually arrived, he found them impossibly difficult. He seemed lost, his heart pounded fiercely, and Tahsina, as though unaware of all this, continued to wash the sticky musk-melon pulp to separate the seeds. He noticed small drops of sweat trickle down her neck as she washed the pulp quite mechanically. Suddenly, she stood up and, as she walked away, she glanced at him and said with seeming innocence, 'It's very hot. Why are you sitting here in this heat?' He had no excuse for sitting in the scorching veranda. He quietly got up, wondering if he should go into the hall or walk out of the house. But before leaving, he called out, 'Tahsina!'

Tahsina stopped.

'Give me some money!'

She walked back to the veranda and entered the room next to it. He followed her and quietly watched her open the trunk in which she kept her money box. Once again, he couldn't turn his gaze away, as the translucent drops of sweat trickled down her neck and the few strands of damp hair that clung to it. Her hands swiftly turned the clothes in the trunk upside down, searching for the money box. She pulled it out from under the clothes, took some money out, and gave it to him; as her long fair fingers brushed his hand, desire instinctively ran through him like an electric charge; his hand trembled; but then, once again, something stopped him; he stood as if paralysed. She quietly locked the trunk and left the room.

He stood in silence for a few seconds in the doorway. His heart, which was beating wildly, slowly regained its normal rhythm. He stepped out of the room into the veranda which was now deserted. Then, he walked out of the house.

The Lal Mandir radiated heat from the distance. The iron pulley which was attached to the dark window high above, and had moved incessantly and noisily all morning and evening, was silent. As he walked out of the temple lane and was passing through the lane with the water tank, a bunch of unruly boys blocked his path. They all looked similar because they had smeared their faces with coal powder. While some had taken off their shirts, the younger ones had shed all their clothes and only wore a black loincloth which was indistinguishable from their skin. They stood in the middle of the street, banged the ground with the heavy sticks they carried in their hands, and shouted:

> *Black sticks, yellow sticks*
> *A cowrie shall get a good harvest*
> *Clouds will come, rains will fall*
> *A cowrie shall turn into fertile soil*
> *And water flow to the harvest.*

They had placed a plate in the middle of the road with a few one-anna coins and some stones, and were urging passers-by to drop a few coins into the plate so they could cook porridge and pray for rains.

The boys allowed him to pass only after he left a coin in the plate. But now his feet refused to move. He stopped and then turned back.

Over dinner in the evening, Badi Apa was again anxious about Zamir, 'Arri, Tahsina, call Zamir so that Bhaiyya can eat his dinner.'

Tahsina walked up to him and gently said, 'Dinner.'

He was drowsy; his head rested on the wicker stool. With his eyes still closed, he mumbled, 'I'm not hungry.'

She was silent.

He then opened his eyes and said, 'I'm not feeling well. I don't want dinner.'

Tahsina quietly turned around and walked back to the big hall.

He was actually unwell. Ammi touched his forehead, checked his wrist, and said, 'His body is warm.'

Tai Amma was not convinced, but she was alarmed when she touched his face and forehead, 'Bahu, the boy's burning with fever.'

Badi Apa also touched his forehead and cheeks and exclaimed, 'Bibi, his temperature is very high.'

'I think it's a heatstroke,' Tai Amma speculated.

'Aji, he had to get a heatstroke,' responded Badi Apa. 'He loafs around all through the afternoon in the loo! He has come here after ages, but hasn't spent a single day with me. Bahu, why did you bring him? He doesn't like being here at all.'

'Bibi, that wasn't the case earlier,' said Tai Amma. 'He used to follow you around all the time calling out—Badi Apa! Badi Apa!'

'Bahannu, he has changed after going away from here.' And then, Badi Apa calmly asked, 'Tahsina, are there a few raw mangoes left? Make some juice for Bhaiyya with them.'

His temperature rose. In the beginning, he was unconscious, and when he regained consciousness for a while, he felt that someone was massaging his body. He drifted back into deep slumber.

For two days, he remained unconscious. On the third day, when he regained consciousness, the fever began to subside. He perspired so profusely that his entire body was drenched, and wiping his forehead and neck with the hem of her dupatta had left Badi Apa tired. He still felt as exhausted as before. His head felt light and his throat very sore.

Who knows how Tai Amma, Badi Apa, and Ammi spent their afternoons in the big hall! They always preferred the breeze that filtered through the neem tree in the courtyard to the frilled cloth-fan that swung from the ceiling in the big hall. But as the sun rays became sharper and the loo began to blow, they retreated from the shade of the neem tree into the big hall. But as soon as the sun went down, they were back on the cots in the shade. But he was prohibited from going out till the evening. The door of his room was shut as usual, the khas screens sprinkled with water as always; a ray of light filtered through the ventilator and its golden line in the dark room helped him trace the passage of the sun. Half-asleep, Noory pulled the rope of the fan as she always did—the music of the fan was interrupted every now and then when she nodded off to sleep, only to wake up instantly. Then the fan would resume its usual rhythm. Tahsina stopped massaging his head with kahu oil. Instead, her fingers moved delicately through his thick hair in harmony with the speed of the cloth-fan.

He was delirious. He could only recall, as in a dream, a few bits and pieces, a few faded memories of the last two days when he was unconscious and feeble. A fair hand, with long elegant fingers, placed a thermometer between his lips, then pulled it out, and placed it back in a bright silver case; the sensuous touch of someone softly massaging his forehead; the soothing, steady, gentle music of Tai Amma's silver bangles as she pressed a wet cloth on the palms of his hands and the soles of his feet; he felt that all his senses were engulfed in a sweet intoxicating dream.

After a moment's pause, a pleasant mellow state of dreams spread through his body again. Half-dreaming and half-awake, he longed for those fingers to caress his hair forever. His slumber deepened, a strange peacefulness overwhelmed his senses, and a diaphanous layer of dreams covered his consciousness. Without any intent or purpose, his right hand tenderly clasped the fingers massaging his head. Her hand froze, then relaxed and became responsive. Fire ignited fire. A torrent of passion emerging from some deep unknown depths passed from fingers to fingers. It seemed as if two rivers, which had been flowing separately had broken their banks and begun to flow together, merging into one another. The clasped hands slipped out of his dark hair and moved closer to his lips. Soft, warm fingers shook as they drew closer to the blazing, trembling lips of a body burning with fever. But suddenly, she regained control over her untamed emotions and disengaged herself from the warm embrace. She stood up abruptly and walked away mumbling something.

He heard her footsteps recede and a door open and shut with a bang. His drifted back to sleep, but the dark dreams clouding his mind had dissipated.

Four

When he woke up, it was still dark. Badi Apa was sitting on her prayer-chowki and reciting her prayers in a poignant voice: 'Maula Ali, Wakil Ali, Badshah Ali.' Her voice was so moving that he thought her entire being would slowly melt and dissolve in the soft light of dawn.

When he stepped out for a morning walk after many days of illness, everything looked fresh and pristine. A bucket was lowered by the pulley outside the mysterious window near the Lal Mandir. It fell into the dark well with a splash; it was then pulled up and filled to the brim with water before it disappeared behind the window. Since the shops in the thathetri wali lane were not yet open, there was silence everywhere. Except for a sweeper-woman, who was raising so much dust that it covered the entire lane in a thin layer of haze. He walked across the metalled road with countless potholes till he reached the tall red brick chimney at the edge of the basti. It was summer and the chimney was no longer bellowing smoke. The chimney had always marked for him the moment when night departed and the new day arrived. He walked up to it and then turned back. He retraced his steps over the same rough and broken roads he had left behind; dust rose at every step he took across them. When he saw the grounds of his old school, he turned into the lane leading up to it. His feet sank into mounds of dust as he walked across the path to reach the boundary wall of the school.

The school was a basti of silence. From a distance, it looked as if it was made of a low-tiled roof over an unending corridor with red-brick archways linked to each other. But as he drew closer, the building was much larger and bigger—the long corridor, the high arches, and the tall glass doors and windows that were surrounded by vast stretches of football and hockey grounds whose boundaries were marked by goalposts. The classrooms were locked, the corridors empty, and the grounds silent. The school was closed. The town's noisy and lively inhabitants migrated to other places every summer, leaving it forlorn. He was familiar both with the sound and the silence. During vacations, when he used to go for a morning walk with Abba Mian, he had often slipped away to pluck flowers from the school's garden. Though he was familiar with every sensation and smell of the school, he had felt like a stranger in a basti whose inhabitants had either abandoned it out of fear of the devil, or had been made invisible by some black magic. He used to walk around the fields, touch and shake the white goalposts, loiter in the empty corridors, gaze at the locked classrooms, and sometimes peep though broken glass windows and watch with uncanny fascination light fall on desks placed in semi-dark rooms, then suddenly step back with a start. If he ever found the lock of a classroom broken, afraid and curious, he would nervously push the door open, walk inside, and marvel at the floors, the closed windows, and the ventilators before rushing out in panic without plucking any flowers.

The scent of the past reached him once again and the magic of bygone years resurfaced in his memory. He drifted towards the garden. The trees and bushes were wet with the morning dew, white flowers glowed through the green leaves like silver embellishments, and restless butterflies touched a flower before drifting away in the wind in search of some other home. As his fingers caressed the dew-drenched leaves and flowers, his thoughts travelled back to that other honey-sweet touch; it rejuvenated him and left a strange frisson on his palms and fingers. His handkerchief was now overflowing with flowers. He tied it in a knot and walked out.

Dust, well-trodden footpaths, potholes, barren lands, ridges separating fields, loose gravel, and trails through grass and bushes—his feet were either wet when he walked through dew-drenched grass or covered with dust as he cut across barren fields. When he heard Hira singing, he knew he was close to his own farmland. Walking on a footpath along a ridge separating fields, he found himself near a cluster of neem and khandal trees. As he reached up and broke a neem twig to clean his teeth, he heard a rustling sound in the leaves. A chameleon scampered out of the leaves and jumped onto a thick branch. Zamir dropped the neem twig and stepped back. The chameleon's crested and ridged body became rougher as it bloated and became bigger. Its neck and back turned a bright orange. Zamir's heart began to beat rapidly with fear. The chameleon changed its colour from orange to red and then to green before it disappeared into the leaves again. Its yellow tail was visible briefly before it too vanished.

Zamir felt an uncanny sense of fear, an inexplicable loneliness; a doubt recurring in some corner of his mind that the blood in his body had been drained. He first turned his steps towards the well, but soon changed his mind and walked straight back home. Instead of bushes with yellow and white flowers, wild grass, and gnarled acacia trees with thorns, the ground was now strewn with debris of cement and red bricks. Abba had not yet begun to construct his kothi, but the rubble was the first sign that he would begin soon.

When he reached his home, its outer walls and terrace were suffused with sunlight. But Badi Apa was still sitting on her prayer-chowki in the courtyard and was reciting 'Maula Ali, Wakil Ali, Badshah Ali' in her plaintive voice. Tai Amma had just knelt and bowed in prayer. Ammi was sleeping; her face was covered with a dupatta to keep the flies away. Tahsina was half-awake, though sleep was trying to overpower her. He went to her and placed the handkerchief filled with flowers in her lap. Her drowsiness vanished in an instant. Surprised, she woke up with a start and looked at him puzzled.

'Flowers,' he said, but his heart was pounding madly. He quickly walked towards the veranda.

He pretended to be busy as he walked from the veranda to the empty rooms, the big hall, the room next to it, and then back to the veranda and the hall.

When he came out, the entire courtyard was fragrant with flowers. There were flowers in Tai Amma's snow-white hair, in Badi Apa's ears, and Tahsina was covered with flowers. She had worn them in her ears, stuck them in her hair, and strung them around her neck. Their colours gave a special glow to her face. Bunni was, however, cribbing. She was not satisfied with the flowers in her ears and wanted a string around her neck too.

'No more, you seem obsessed.'

'Baji, just a small string of flowers.'

'There aren't enough left for a small string. If Zamir Bhai brings some more tomorrow, I'll make a string for you,' Tahsina said affectionately. But there was also a pleasant lilt in her voice. Bunni was not convinced by her promise and persisted, 'But you have so many!'

'Not so many! Hardly a few buds are left.' And she pulled back the hem of her dupatta. Bunni was at first cross, then she made an angry face, and when none of her tricks worked, she pounced on Tahsina who had by now spread out her dupatta again and was stringing the remaining flowers. Tahsina immediately gathered the flowers in her dupatta, pushed Bunni aside, and burst out laughing, 'You are crazy!'

Her dupatta slipped from her head and the flowers adorning her knotted hair shimmered like mica and a lock of hair fell over her blushing cheeks. 'Haven't I already promised to make another garland tomorrow? Why don't you listen?' She laughed again, 'What a wild girl!'

'Tahsina, cover your head,' Ammi admonished.

Tahsina was stunned. She covered her head, arranged her dupatta which had slipped down to her shoulders, pushed back the lock of hair falling over her face, and left.

Ammi opened the paandan and began to prepare paan for herself.

'Tai Amma, do you want some paan?'

'Yes, Bahu, a small one,' responded Tai Amma, and Ammi began to prepare it quietly.

Tahsina was lost, Bunni bewildered, and Zamir dazed. He broke into beads of sweat. He understood that Ammi had admonished him instead of Tahsina.

'Aji, all I know is this,' Ammi spoke at last, 'as long I was in my maternal home, my mother never let me even look at flowers. If I ever wore some secretly in my ears, I made sure they were well-covered by my dupatta. I knew that if Ammi had caught sight of them, she would have drunk my blood. But now flowers are in vogue.'

'Yes,' Tai Amma said nostalgically, 'Now every damn sin is in fashion.'

'Yes, unveiling is in fashion, not keeping your head covered is in fashion, low necklines are in fashion. These girls have no shame. It was never so in our days.'

'You were only born yesterday, Bibi,' Tai Amma added. 'In our times, we observed such strict purdah that no strange men even heard our voices. My Badi Amma, may Allah rest her soul in peace, was very pious. Even after her hair had turned grey, the water carrier couldn't catch a glimpse of her toe rings. Bibi, in those days, we observed purdah even in front of our parents. You know, Buniyad Ali's sister, the unlucky one—her father summoned physicians and hakims, but she refused to give up her purdah and her condition continued to deteriorate till her pretty face was hidden under the veil of dust. No man, neither a member of the family nor a stranger, ever caught sight of her face.'

Tahsina quietly got up and walked towards the kitchen. Astounded and bewildered, Bunni too followed her.

Ammi's watchful gaze followed Tahsina till she entered the kitchen.

'Bibi, 1 don't care what people say,' Ammi's face was flushed with anger, 'I don't like this shamelessness.'

'What is there to dislike about it?' Tai Amma responded. 'You are not an outsider. And you didn't say anything you shouldn't have. You noticed something that was not right and pointed it out. That's it. That's what elders are for.'

Ammi said, 'Tai Amma, I'm afraid my words have been misunderstood. After all, she is a grown-up girl. But tell me, am I wrong when I say that her eyes are without shame and she walks without any modesty? She walks with her head held high and her chest out. Once or twice I thought of telling her—Beti, grown-up girls walk with drooping shoulders, but then I said to myself, why should I bother and earn everyone's curses for no reason?'

'But, Bibi, that's totally unfair. One doesn't behave like a stranger with one's own people.'

'Tai Amma, this is not about behaving like a stranger. The matter of an unwed girl is delicate. It's only the mother's gaze that can set her right. When Badi Apa is there, why should I point fingers at Tahsina? It's her duty to keep Tahsina in check.'

'Ari, ever since Abba Mian passed away, Chhammo has lost her mind. She neither rebukes Tahsina, nor gives her advice.

Ammi didn't say anything for a while. She pulled the tray of betel nuts towards her and began to chop them. Then, she added meditatively, 'All I know is that Badi Apa should marry her off now.'

Tai Amma was quiet for a while and then said slowly, 'Buniyad Ali has written another letter.'

Ammi was alarmed. 'Really? Badi Apa didn't mention it.'

'She will. This time she'll have to.'

'Why?' Ammi became alert.

'This time they want a clear answer—yes or no. We must decide.'

Both Ammi and Tai Amma were thoughtful for a few moments. Then, Tai Amma said, as if talking to herself, 'They are right. After all, how long can they wait? If you agree, then go ahead. Do it or else let it be.'

'What's going on in Badi Apa's mind? Do you have a clue?' Ammi asked.

'Bibi, I don't have a clue. When Abba Mian was alive, Buniyad Ali sent letter after letter, but Abba Mian refused to reply. Chhammo too kept very quiet. Days have passed in silence, and with each passing day the girl is getting older.' Tai Amma paused and then resumed, 'Now her brother has come; I think she'll consult him.'

'When has she consulted her brother about anything in the past?' Ammi's tone was sharp.

'This time she surely will.' Tai Amma paused and declared, 'And the truth is, she loves her brother a lot. She always longs to meet him and talk to him.'

Ammi was quiet. She placed the nut-cracker back in the tray, mixed the chopped betel nuts, and then, placing some in her palms, tossed them into her mouth. She sighed and said, 'Bhai, this is between brother and sister, who am I to poke my nose in it? But shouldn't I say what I really think? Did she consult her brother when Tahsina was betrothed to Imdad?'

'Yes, what you say is true,' Tai Amma responded. 'But it is also true, Bibi, that Tahsina's father was alive at that time. Who'd have paid poor Chhammo any attention?'

Ammi was silent again. She chewed and chewed the betel nuts and then spoke, 'Tai Amma, the problem is that she has left the matter to her daughter, and I say that's how it should be. If tomorrow, God forbid, she doesn't like the groom, she shouldn't blame Badi Apa for having dumped her in hell.' Ammi was quiet, but she hadn't yet finished.

After a few seconds' pause, she spoke again, though this time in a hushed voice, 'Why is the girl so sullen all the time?'

'Ai, her cursed mother is also like that,' Tai Amma answered casually.

'Tai Ammi, this one is surly all the time. Who knows what sorrow has stricken her? Our Badi Apa is so lost in herself that she rarely pays attention to anything.'

Tai Amma suddenly got up, 'Oh no, it's sunny here now.' The sunlight had crept up to the cot.

'Let's go inside.' Ammi too stood up and said, 'Zamir, come inside.'

He moved to the room next to the hall. He came out of the room many times during the afternoon—sometimes to drink water, sometimes on the pretext of going to the bathroom. He walked through the veranda, from there to the courtyard, and then back through the veranda. The veranda remained deserted that afternoon. Tahsina neither came out to dye the dupattas, nor to wash musk-melon seeds.

Then he dozed off. When he woke up and came to the courtyard, the sun had set. Ammi, Tai Amma, and Badi Apa were all sitting outside.

'Zamir, come. The breeze is very pleasant,' Badi Apa called to him. He walked to the courtyard and sat on the stool under the neem tree.

'Ai, Chhammo, you spoke too soon, the wind has dropped again.' The fan in Tai Amma's hand began to spin faster.

The air was very still. The back of Zamir's shirt was soaked with sweat.

'Behna, it's very hot. My entire body is covered with prickly heat,' Ammi said.

Tai Amma began to grumble, 'Tauba, tauba, the sky has turned copper-red. Damn, it's raining fire!'

Then suddenly, her tone changed and she began to pray, 'Ilahi, for the sake of your beloved Mohammad, send some rain…rain…send rain for the sake of thirsty souls of Karbala…'

Badi Apa said, 'Bahannu, they say the astrologers have predicted that there'll be no rain this year.'

Tai Amma instantly countered, 'No, Bibi, don't say such things. May God have mercy!'

Ammi muttered, 'Aji, we have landed ourselves in trouble by coming here. It was never so hot in the past. Spring is almost over and there is no sign of a cloud in the sky.'

'Ari, Bibi,' Tai Amma's imagination ran wild, 'this drought is nothing compared to that one…but you and I were not even born then...Badi Amma used to tell us about it...the entire monsoon season passed and there was not a drop of rain...Ashadh passed by without rain. Sawan was dry, so was Bhadon...the sky was copper-red...the earth was parched...the trees pined for a drop of water, cattle bellowed all night because of thirst...So, Bibi, that year not a seed sprouted... there was famine...everyone frantically called for help... the cursed mothers sold their children for a fistful of gram and their daughters for a morsel of food...there was such a slaughter of animals that even crows were killed.'

'Even crows? Ai, Tai Amma, what are you saying?' Badi Apa's eyes were wide open.

'Yes, Bibi, crows....' Tai Amma sounded terrified. 'Crows...Bibi, it was not just an ordinary famine, it was *azab-i-Ilahi*, a curse of God. When the famine ended, there was news of theft every day; robbers struck first in one mohalla and then in some village. Ai Mian, as if that wasn't enough, a mutiny broke out. The earth trembled. Cannons and gunfire reduced huge havelis to rubble, and the people who lived in them were left with no shelter. And Mian, Badi Amma told us that the fight for Dilli was so ferocious that its wells were filled with rubble and the Jamuna had turned red with blood.'

Tai Amma was silent for some time. She had strayed into such a strange world that her voice failed her. Badi Apa was entranced. There was terror in her eyes. Ammi too was quiet, but then she fidgeted where she sat and tried to break the spell Tai Amma had cast on her. 'Well, what can one say about Dilli? That city has the blessings of a fakir. It has been ruined many times, but has flourished each time.'

Tai Ammi continued to gaze at Zamir. She was herself lost in the spell she had woven. Then she began to fan herself, and mumbled, 'Call it a fakir's blessing or a curse for our sins. All I know is this that in the abode of twenty-two saints, no empire has flourished beyond a hundred years. Every hundred years, the rulers change and the subjects are exiled.'

'Thank God!' Badi Apa was jubilant, as there was a rustle of neem leaves and a gentle breeze caressed scorched bodies. Suddenly, a shadow passed over the courtyard burnt by the setting sun. It was as if the sunlight had acquired feet and had quickly climbed up the front wall, reached the terrace, slid past the attic on the top floor, and disappeared.

'Allah, send some rain!' Badi Apa's pleading eyes rose towards the sky.

Small patches of clouds drifting in the wind grew closer and merged. They continued to float as the parched courtyard came alive. The clouds scattered again and the sunlight returned to the attic, slid down the boundary wall, descended from wall to wall, and spread once more over the courtyard.

An ikka clattered to a stop outside the entrance door.

'Who could have come in that ikka?' Badi Apa was surprised.

Ammi turned to Zamir and said, 'Go and see who has come in that ikka.' Then she announced to Badi Apa, 'I think your brother has come. The lawsuit ended today.'

Zamir got up and walked towards the entrance door.

Badi Apa was praying nervously, 'Ilahi, have mercy, may there be some good tidings!'

When Zamir reached the front door, Baba was getting down from the ikka. His grey hair was covered with dust and his face revealed the fatigue of the journey. Baba paid the ikkawallah, handed over the bags to the servant, and walked in to the house with heavy steps. Zamir followed him. When he stepped inside the house, all eyes, filled with expectation and hope, were raised towards him. Baba took out a handkerchief from his pocket, wiped the dust off his clothes, cleaned his face, mopped the sweat flowing down the nape of his neck, and sat down on the stool. Badi Apa came and stood behind him with her fan.

'Bhaiyya, what happened?' Tai Amma asked nervously.

'The judgment has been passed.'

'Judgment...'

The vigorously whirling fan suddenly stopped and then began to move intermittently and slowly. There was silence for a few minutes except for the sound of the fan in Badi Apa's hand which moved slowly. Baba rose and walked towards the bathroom.

After a bath, he came out in a chequered tahmat and a white vest, sat on the stool, and pulled the freshly prepared huqqa toward him. Badi Apa, Tai Amma, and Ammi sat, dazed like statues. The sun had gone down. Evening shadows and a little sprinkling of water had awakened the suppressed heat of the earth, and steam rose from the damp earth.

Baba pulled the huqqa a little towards himself and once again began to puff at it. The fatigue and anxiety, visible on his face when he had got off the ikka, was washed away. The fragrance of the fresh earth and the soothing gurgling sound of the huqqa were so blissful that his eyes began to droop.

The music of the huqqa and Baba's closed eyes left Ammi, Badi Apa, and Tai Amma speechless. Zamir felt suffocated in that silence. He wanted to sneak out and leave, but he couldn't gather the courage to do so. Finally, when he decided to stealthily slip out of that oppressive atmosphere, he heard the sound of wailing. Badi Apa had been controlling herself for a long time. She broke down and, hiding her head between her knees, began to sob. Baba opened his eyes, looked at Badi Apa, closed his eyes once again, and the gurgling sound of huqqa resumed with the same rhythm as before.

The people in the haveli slept early that night. The big lamp which always burned late into the night, and in whose light Baba used to pour over Bade Abba's yellowed, worn-out papers in the courtyard or on the terrace or inside the hall, was not lit that evening.

Those who walked past the haveli got the impression that everyone had gone out for the night to attend a function.

Five

Ashadh was desolate, Sawan was dry, and now Bhadon too was passing by. Clouds gathered in the sky and drifted away; stray clouds, glowing in the sunlight, wandered from one end to the other aimlessly; dirty rags of dark clouds merged briefly, threw a veil over the sun, and chased the sunshine away from the fields to a place beyond the trees, and then vanished; thick clusters of clouds floated in from all directions, paused, and then glided past.

'Today there are clouds in the sky,' a passer-by remarked.

Gandal looked at the sky and said matter-of-factly, 'It won't rain.'

Light and dark clouds passed overhead. There was no thunder or rain and the sky was clear once again.

'That twittering cry of the sandpiper means it will rain,' Tai Amma said optimistically on hearing the sandpiper's long tweets.

'Tai Amma,' Bunni asked, 'why does a sandpiper twitter so loudly?'

'Beti, it begs for water and summons the clouds.'

'Do the clouds give her water then?' Achhe's imagination strayed.

'Yes, the wretched one is very unlucky. She did not fetch water for her brother, and so she was cursed and turned into a sandpiper. She cannot drink a drop of water with her beak. There's a hole in her head; when it rains the water drips through it into her parched throat; then she is thirsty again.'

The sandpiper kept pleading for water, invoking clouds, rattling at noontime, and shrieking in the dead of the night, but there was not a drop of rain. The dry, scorching afternoons were heavy with dust and the stars at night seemed dirty. There was neither rain nor a hint of rain—neither the pitter-patter of Sawan, nor the heavy showers of Bhadon; unlike the year before, when reddish mangoes were sold cheaply, there were none this year; there were no berries of Bhadon either; there was neither the scent of the damp earth nor the stench of the wet garbage heaps.

Every morning the sky was covered with dust. He woke up and walked to his farmland. Baba led and he followed. As soon as they entered the fields, Gandal appeared from somewhere behind a tree and followed them along a path and, coming closer, quietly announced, 'Sarkar, the bitter-gourd has withered.'

Gandal and Hira used to wake up at dawn and fetch water from the well all day and all night. The sandpiper's twitter and Hira's singing could be heard in the sweltering afternoons, in the still of the night, when the bell tolled in the morning, and as the sunlight retreated behind the first ridge and then the next. But the earth remained thirsty and in the grip of hot dusty winds. Every day, Gandal announced that some crop or the other had been ruined.

'Sarkar…the corn is destroyed…the red storm raged yesterday.'

Baba rearranged his spectacles, coughed, and said softly, 'Okay,' and walked past the well towards the fields.

'Bibi, when I looked out, I saw that the sky was blood red like a piece of flesh, and the walls were red as flames,' Badi Apa said. She was terrified, 'Tai Amma, I've never seen such a storm in my lifetime!'

'No, Bibi, nor have I,' Tai Amma replied. 'Yes, Badi Amma used to tell us that before the mutiny, there was such a storm; the sky was so red that it seemed to drip with blood; the walls, the parapets, and the attic were red, as though someone had smeared red powder on them.'

'Bahannu, all I know is this,' sorrow had replaced terror in Badi Apa's voice, 'ever since the foundation of this damn kothi was dug, we have faced some calamity or the other every day.'

Tai Amma instantly supported her, 'You are right, Chhammo! When Shabbir Hussain had broached the subject with Abba Mian, he had refused outright, saying we will not touch that land; it is jinxed and it will not flourish.'

'Tai Amma, you are very superstitious!' Ammi said, 'Bhai, it all depends on the situation; things go right at times and wrong at other times. When it works, you call it luck, and when it doesn't, you say it is jinxed.'

Tai Amma answered, 'Bahu, neither you nor your husband ever listen to us. All right, Bibi, we are fools.' Tai Amma began to sulk quietly.

Badi Apa's mind wandered off. As if recalling a dream, she said, 'Abba Mian had someone else with him…I thought it was Mir Bu Ali…Abba Mian and Bade Abba looked worried…then Mir Bu Ali screamed, the haveli's beam has collapsed…then I woke up.'

Tai Amma was shaken. She gazed into the vacant space for some time. Then turning to one side, she sighed, 'Some dreams actually come true.'

Tai Amma was quiet after this. No one said anything for some time. Ammi and Badi Apa continued to sit like statues.

When Tai Amma spoke again, her tone was bitter, 'Now build your damn kothi, the haveli has been lost.'

In response, Badi Apa said with a sigh, 'Yes Bahannu.' She didn't say anything more. The construction of the kothi had begun. Visits to the police station and courts were done with. Abba Mian's letters were once again bundled up and carefully locked away in the wooden box full of books. Now, Baba's days were spent at his farmland. Ammi had dragged Zamir into this wrangle, 'Aji, how long will you look after everything alone! Consider your age. If you collapse, you'll be bedridden for good and will never be able to get up. What does Zamir do the whole day at home? Why don't you ask him to look after the work?'

Even if Zamir had stayed back at home, what difference would it have made? The veranda was deserted all afternoon, the courtyard was hot, and the branches of the neem tree either swayed desultorily or drooped. Tahsina was everywhere—in the veranda, in the courtyard, near the flower bed. But as soon as he caught sight of her, she seemed to disappear. Ammi kept a watchful eye on her all the time. Sleeping or awake, Tahsina was conscious that Ammi's critical eyes followed her. Zamir felt suffocated at home. But there was no relief outside either. There were gunny bags full of cement all over the place, heaps of red grit, and wet mortar which the labourers filled in large metal containers and carried on their heads towards the half-built walls. They climbed bamboo ladders to reach the raised platforms, emptied their containers, and returned. And then there were the donkeys loaded with sacks full of red-brick—rows and rows of them kept coming and going the whole day. It seemed as if a city was being built, not a small kothi. A continuously moving caravan of donkeys, the crushing of granite stones for the road, the music of handsaws at work, labourers, and the steadily rising walls—he found the bustle jarring and purposeless.

'Zamir Mian, we can't make the beams?'

'Why not?'

The old carpenter adjusted his spectacles and said, 'The logs that arrived yesterday are missing.'

'The logs are missing?'

How could the logs be missing? Each and every one was questioned. Reprimanded. Labourers left their work and gathered around Zamir. They began to blame each other. Then Baba came. The noisy labourers suddenly became quiet. Baba asked straightforward questions. One labourer answered rudely. Everyone suspected him. He was dismissed.

The logs for the beams and the door frames were stolen. Then there was suspicion that some bricks had disappeared. A few gunny sacks of cement too went missing. Whoever came within the circle of doubt was dismissed. Thefts continued, and so did the dismissal of labourers. But the labourers were all the same. Those dismissed were re-employed. They were dismissed again and again and then called back to work, creating a cycle of spite.

'Why hasn't the work begun yet?'

'Zamir Mian, treasure!' one labourer answered in a hushed voice.

'Treasure? What treasure?'

'Aji, there was a metallic sound while we were digging near the roots of the neem tree in the veranda. Now everyone is digging there…they will find treasure.'

The labourers dug deeper and deeper near the neem tree all through the day. They kept deepening the pit. Those who did not participate in the digging sat nearby, wavering between hope and doubt. There were cries of amazement at every blow of the spade.

In the evening, they found a copper pot filled with coal.

'Ashrafis turned into coal,' Tai Amma mourned. 'Aji, it's all a matter of luck and, Bibi, it's also about intentions. This happened due to the evil eye of some labourer.'

The evil eye of the labourer was never neutralised; nor was the unpleasantness.

Zamir felt nervous when the labourers spoke harshly and retreated to the shade of the banyan tree near the well.

Gandal called, 'Hira, O Hira…Hira, where are you?'

'Here.'

'Oye, Chhote Mian has come, bring out the cot.'

'Coming!'

Hira jumped from embankment to embankment and came running. A string cot was placed under the banyan tree.

How comforted he felt lying under its dense shade! Gandal dug out some cow-dung cakes buried under ash, broke them with his tongs, filled his chillum, and sat on the edge of the cot near Zamir's feet to smoke his huqqa.

'Zamir Mian,' Hira said.

'Yes, what!'

'When will the kothi be ready?'

'The construction is going on. It'll be ready soon.'

'After that, will all of us live in the haveli?'

'Where else?'

'And the haveli will be vacant?'

Gandal, whose eyes were drooping as he smoked his chillum, opened his eyes, cleared his throat, and passed the chillum to Hira. Then his eyes began to droop again. He began to hum:

Hira, you wasted your nights in sleep, your days in eating,
Your life was priceless, you exchanged it for nothing.

Zamir's eyes too were drooping and a sweet drowsiness was spreading through his body when Munshiji's voice startled him.

'Zamir Mian,' Munshiji sounded nervous.

He opened his eyes, 'What?'

'The well is dry.'

'The well is dry?' He was amazed.

'Yes,' Munshiji said, 'the well is dry. Where can we get water now? The work has stopped.'

Zamir stood up. He first went to the well where all the labourers had gathered leaving their work. Some were peering into the well. Some were sitting in groups under a tree and smoking a huqqa. He decided to go back home.

When he opened the door of the big hall and went in, Baba looked at him puzzled and Badi Apa irritably asked, 'Ai hai, why are you loitering around in such heat? Just look at his face; it has turned red.'

Baba ignored Badi Apa and, fixing his gaze on him, asked, 'What has happened?'

'The work has stopped,' he replied in a low voice.

'Why?' Baba urged.

'The small well is dry.'

'How?' Badi Apa was startled.

Her question remained unanswered. He wanted to respond, but looking at Baba's face, he kept quiet.

Baba quietly got up, changed his clothes, put on his shoes, and went out.

The silence broke.

Tai Amma teased, 'Ai Zamir, is the small well really dry?'

'Yes, Tai Amma.'

'How?' Badi Apa wondered.

'Because of the heat.'

'Because of the heat?' Tai Amma taunted. 'When do wells dry in the summer? After all, there is a well at the rahat also. That has water all-round-the-clock. Why isn't it dry?'

'Tai Amma,' he explained, 'This small well was dug for temporary use. It was kachha and shallow. It dried because it has been exceptionally hot.'

She muttered, 'Yes, you'll say anything now.'

There was a long silence.

Then Ammi yawned and said, 'Every damn thing is going wrong. Nothing seems to get done on time. Each day there's a new crisis.'

Neither Badi Apa nor Tai Amma said anything in response. After some time, Tai turned to Badi Apa and said, 'Chhammo, remember when Pirjiwalah's house was being constructed?

'Yes,' Badi Apa answered, absent-mindedly.

'They purchased land with a lot of fanfare,' Tai Amma said mockingly. 'God, how they boasted! As though theirs was the first house to be built! The neem tree was chopped down and a small well was dug. Pirji distributed sweets. Everyone in the community was invited to the function. They ate the sweets and drank glasses full of water from the well. The water was so sweet, so cool, that I can't describe it.' She paused, and then began again, 'Bibi...on the third day, when the water carrier dropped his bucket into the well to draw water, the drum crashed to the floor of the well. The well was dry.'

Badi Apa gazed at Tai Amma's face.

Ammi said thoughtfully, 'Aji, Tai Amma, it all has to do with evil intentions. And those damn Pirjiwalahs are crooks.'

'That is true, Bahu,' Tai Amma responded, 'but there are also plots of land that never flourish. Pirji tried everything he could. He even dug a second well, but there were so many problems that the house was never built...At about the same time, his grandson, an impressive youth with a broad chest and a strong body, fell ill suddenly...and died the same year.'

Badi Apa was silent.

Ammi began to reflect and then added morosely, 'Anyway, Tai Amma, don't say such things. That house was built. It is so magnificent that no other house in the city can match it.'

'Built? Do you call it a home?' Tai Amma responded nonchalantly, 'When the damn house was built, the family was destroyed. The elder son died; the father passed away; the younger one somehow survived to complete it. Now, you may say that there is nothing to match it, but does it have the feathers of Surkhab? Its design is not half as lovely as the one Pirji had prepared.'

Ammi was speechless. Badi Apa sat quietly. Then she remembered that it was time for namaz.

The mortar lying in the open under the scorching sun had become solidified. Its upper layer had hardened into a crust and had begun to crack. Yellow wasps that used to hover over it all day had migrated. Baba gave up the idea of another well and started making arrangements for a handpump. The construction work stopped. The installation of the handpump began. Yellow mortar turned into a dry heap. Half-built walls that needed to be moistened frequently began to crumble. Masons and labourers who had carried the bricks all day and built the walls left the building unfinished. There was a sense of paralysis everywhere. Labourers worked near the dry well, and all one could see at first were long iron rods tied with a rope stuck in the ground. Then the rods disappeared. And, in their place, a short and squat handpump appeared. The pump began to work. Mortar was moistened and remixed. Water was sprinkled on the half-raised walls again. Even the yellow wasps, which had migrated because the ground was stone-dry, came back to the swamp near the handpump.

The handpump worked noisily all day, and there was a continuous hustle and bustle near the walls. Zamir sometimes kept a watch on the newly built structure and on the rooms where the rubble was dumped. At times, when he was sick and tired of all the activity, he walked away from the clutter of bricks and stone to sleep under the tranquil shade of the banyan tree, lulled into slumber by the soft gurgling sound of Gandal's huqqa.

Hira, you wasted your nights in sleep and your days in eating.

Your life was priceless, you exchanged it for nothing.

Hira looked at his cracked feet, his bruised fingers, and the palms of his hands chaffed by the rope of the well, and said, 'Gandal, what is God's will? Will it rain this time?'

Gandal coughed and puffed his chillum.

Hira sat quietly for a while and then began to mutter, 'What a Sawan! I haven't sung the Alha even once.'

Bunni and Achhe sneaked out of the haveli and roamed about all over the fields. They suddenly emerged from somewhere and called out, 'Zamir Bhai, look. We have caught a butterfly.'

'Butterfly, O butterfly, convey my salaam to Allah Mian!'

'And mine too!' Achhe added.

'Butterfly, O butterfly, convey my salaam to Allah Mian and Achhe's too!'

And the butterfly escaped from the clutches of Bunni's small hands and began to float in the air.

Zamir reprimanded them, 'Why are you wandering in the sun...come here!'

Both stopped, looked at each other, and then ran away shouting, 'Zamir Bhai, we are going home!'

Bunni and Achhe disappeared from his sight, and he got back to work. Later, he went to lie down under the shade of the banyan tree. Just as his eyes began to close, Bunni and Achhe reappeared. This time, they were terrified.

'Zamir Bhai, a chameleon!'

'There!' Achhe pointed to the khandal tree. 'On the khandal tree. It turned red when it saw us.'

'So, you didn't go home?' He glared at them and they both froze.

Then Zamir chased them home. They ran across the fields, footpaths, barren lands, metalled roads, dusty lanes, and small markets; they ran past the water tank and the Lal Mandir till they reached the haveli with its scorching courtyard and the deserted veranda with bees hovering in a corner. Zamir's heart beat rapidly as he stepped into the house. Then, as he became despondent again, he turned around and went back to his fields.

Six

The construction of the kothi continued intermittently. It had to be stopped for a short while, and then begun again. Baba's calculations, both about the time and the expenditure, were slightly off the mark.

It had already cost more than twice the expected amount, and the construction was nowhere near completion. Zamir's vacations were about to end. He was sceptical about whether he would be allowed to continue with his studies or not. While Ammi taunted him or tried to provoke him, Baba's silences were disturbing. Ammi spoke on different occasions in different tones, but she only harped on one point. Once she told Tai Amma, 'Aji, Tai Amma, studies should end with a BA degree. Why show off with an MA? I have been urging him to stop. Now that you have done your BA, you will get a job if you are lucky. Would a damn MA add some Surkhab feathers?' Sometimes she tried to reason with him, 'Bhaiyya, give up your studies and do some useful work. Your father is a pensioner and is old. People pray for a son so that his earnings can support them in their old age. But your studies don't seem to end. You are no longer a kid that I have to explain everything to you. See for yourself, look at our situation. So much money went down the drain on the lawsuit and we ended up losing the haveli also. This damn kothi is costing a lot of money and will never be finished. There is no income other than the pension. How can we continue to pay for your studies?' Ammi chided him often, while he quietly listened. Baba always remained silent. But then, one day he declared, 'Finish your studies and get a job!' He didn't preach, plead, or ask him for his opinion. He only told him to leave right away, collect his certificate from the college, and go with the letters of recommendation he had himself written to meet a few officers who were obliged to him and ask for a job. But suddenly, Ammi remembered that they had to shift to the kothi, and one man alone could not do it. That made sense to Baba. Zamir's departure was postponed by a couple of days, and they began shifting to the new house even before it was completed.

Zamir didn't sleep till late that night. Tai Amma finished her Isha prayers before lying down on the cot in the middle of the courtyard. Achhe and Bunni demanded that she tell them a story. She began to tell them a story about an exiled prince and an unfortunate princess. Before the story reached its end, Bunni had dozed off. Then Achhe's eyes too began to droop. Tai Amma continued with her story and, when her listeners started snoring, she too went to sleep. Usually, Baba was always relaxed at night. He would sit quietly on a stool in his tahmat and muslin kurta and smoke his huqqa for such a long time that Zamir would never get to know when he moved to his cot and went to sleep. But tonight Zamir was still awake when Baba put his huqqa aside, lay down on his cot, and went to sleep. Tahsina quietly got up, reduced the flame of the lantern, and went back to her cot. The night was humid. The stars, which had earlier looked like dirty, dust-covered discs, suddenly sparkled. At last, Badi Apa too, who had been sitting in the same posture on her mat since the Isha prayers, telling her beads, got up. The low flame in the lantern was about to go out. She quickly moved forward and raised the wick, but the flame began to splutter. She picked up the lantern and shook it to see if it had enough oil.

She called out, 'Tahsina!'

'Yes.'

'Bibi, didn't you put oil in the lantern?'

'I did,' Tahsina paused and added hesitantly, 'but there was very little oil in the bottle.'

Badi Apa put the lantern back on the stool and began to grumble, 'Now, we'll spend the whole night in the dark.'

The night was pitch-dark, cool, and moist; unblemished by the light from the lantern. A dust-free, stainless, dark night. Tai Amma was snoring. Badi Apa too dozed off. Heavy with sleep, Zamir's eyes began to shut.

When his eyes opened, he saw the same morning routine—Badi Apa sitting on her chowki, reciting in her poignant, heart-rending voice, 'Maula Ali, Wakil Ali, Badshah Ali.'

His eyes began to shut once again. He felt as though the sound of lamentation was coming from somewhere beyond the boundary of sleep:

It's not my practice to give sermons or preach
But I have heard you are compassionate.
My means are few and my work has stopped,
But, O Maula, my heart has gathered all its strength.
Because you are obliging, O Mushkil Kusha Ali
Maula Ali, Wakil Ali, Badshah Ali.

Ammi shook him, 'Zamir, get up. At least on days when there is work, you should get up early. Sleeping daily till twelve o'clock…like some damn opium addict!'

He jumped up and got to his feet. When he looked around, the courtyard seemed transformed. All kinds of old and new junk, which had been locked in the halls and rooms, was now piled up in the courtyard.

Bade Abba's drawing-room door was also open. Zamir saw the red and grey chillums, carved with fine lattice work in gold and yellow, neatly laid out in rows. There was a thick layer of dust on them. A dazzling brass spittoon and a walking stick in the shape of Urdu letter 'Laam' stood in a corner. He noticed the long and broad wooden cot covered with a sparkling white sheet, a rug, and a bolster pillow. An unlit huqqa stood next to the bed. A heavy cloth-fan with frills hung from hooks fixed on the wooden beams on the roof. It seemed as though Abba Mian would walk in any time, recline on the bolster, and the cloth-fan would begin to swing again till every corner of the drawing room became cool.

'Tai Amma,' Badi Apa said sorrowfully, 'It seems as though Abba Mian has just gone out for a while to the mosque.' Badi Apa's voice was choked. She grew quiet. Her eyes filled with tears. She went out silently.

A wealth of other things had emerged from the dark rooms, cellars, and locked boxes, and were heaped in the courtyard: rusted vessels, mouldering papers which had not seen sunlight for ages, old, moth-eaten clothes which fell apart at the slightest touch, and souvenirs and memorabilia of ancestors which had been locked up in wooden boxes for generations and whose caretakers and descendants had never seen them.

'Ai, Badi Apa, what's wrong with you?' Ammi came out to inspect the hall and small rooms. Her hair, face, and clothes were all covered with dust and wet with sweat. She was surprised to see Badi Apa sitting comfortably, 'Ai, Badi Apa, what's wrong with you? You are sitting as though there is no work. Why don't you take care of your luggage? When will it be packed and when will it be carted away?'

'Bibi, why bother about me? You take care of your own luggage,' Badi Apa whimpered.

'Ai hai, what's happened now?' Ammi snapped.

'What can happen?' Badi Apa tried to sound casual, but her tone betrayed a tinge of disappointment and protest. 'You pack your luggage and send it.'

'And what about yours?' Ammi asked irritably.

'My things will not go.'

'Why?' Ammi was stunned.

Baba was standing near the pile of luggage and arranging it. He turned around to see what was happening. He walked up to them quietly.

Ammi instantly appealed to him, 'Ji, do you hear? Badi Apa says her luggage will not go.'

'Why?...What's the matter, Badi Apa?'

'I will not go,' Badi Apa declared firmly.

Ammi was quiet. Then Baba asked gently, 'But why, after all?'

'You can't force me. You go. May Allah bless you in your new house! I will not go.'

'Tai Amma, do you see?' Ammi appealed to Tai Amma for justice.

Tai Amma admonished Badi Apa, 'Ai, Chhammo! What's the matter with you? How can you decide not to go! What'll you do here alone? Break your head against the wall?'

Ammi promptly added, 'And who is going to let you stay here alone?'

'Aji, what difference will it make if I stay here? Tahsina will go to some stranger's home. It's only a matter of days. Let Bhai Buniyad Ali come, I will have her nikah performed and send her away. As for Bunni, she is attached to Tai Amma and can go with her. That leaves only me. I'll request the new occupants to let me linger on in a cell here.'

'Badi Apa, why are you talking like an idiot?' Ammi tried to reason with her. 'Say something that makes sense. When you have your own house, why burden others? Don't humiliate your own brother.'

Badi Apa refused to budge. Ammi, Tai Amma, and Baba were silent. Ammi turned and addressed him, 'Zamir, go and get Badi Apa's things.'

'No, don't take my luggage,' Badi Apa said firmly.

'But why?' Baba asked with the same firmness.

'I will not leave this place.' Badi Apa decided to confront Baba too.

'But why won't you go? What's the reason?' Baba was impatient now.

'I won't go,' Badi Apa fumed, but the very next moment sounded sad. 'Now only my dead body will leave the haveli.... Abba Mian closed his eyes here; I too…' Badi Apa broke into tears.

Baba quietly slipped away, went back to the piled up luggage, and began to arrange it.

'Zamir.'

'Yes?'

'One pushcart has been loaded. You go along with it.'

When he went out, a pushcart was actually at the door loaded with luggage. Bunni and Achhe impatiently walked up to the pushcart driver, urged him to move, and then ran to the other side of the cart and tried to push it with all their might. Their faces turned red, but the cart did not move. At Zamir's request, the cart driver pushed the cart loaded with luggage tied down with ropes, and moved out of the haveli.

Rows of carts carried luggage from the haveli to the kothi all day. Luggage from the haveli was unloaded in the veranda and in the rooms of the kothi in which the cement on the walls had not yet dried. Achhe and Bunni walked like leaders before each pushcart and, as it drew near the kothi, they ran ahead to announce its arrival. Zamir impatiently dragged the little leaders out of the way and helped to unload the carts. Bunni and Achhe led the procession of carts, but at times they ran up the stairs of the kothi and stood on the terrace to announce their arrival as they crawled across the fields, 'Zamir Bhai, a cart is coming.' When the cart arrived, they ran down from the terrace to welcome it. Leaders, announcers, receptionists—

and then, bored with all this business, they chased a butterfly which fluttered up in the air and disappeared.

The luggage was piled so high that it almost touched the roof of the veranda: tables, chairs, bedposts, string cots, large trunks, locked wooden boxes, half-wound reels of rope, large vessels, small pots, a long bamboo stick, odd wooden legs and boards, spools of tape, a sagging string cot, empty canisters, old and new tin cans, metal containers dented out of shape, and an empty boot-polish box with a parrot painted on it—useless perhaps, but very much a part of the luggage. Zamir began to feel claustrophobic. It seemed as if the luggage would fall over his head. He walked out and went towards the well. The well was silent. The pulleys were motionless. The bulls sat lazily on one side. Gandal was sitting under the banyan tree smoking his huqqa.

'Gandal, didn't you draw water from the well today?'

'No, Mian,' Gandal said. 'The rats and birds made a hole in the bucket. Hira has gone to get it welded.'

Gandal got up and brought a cot for Zamir. 'Chhote Mian, sit!'

Zamir sat down. Gandal brought some dung-cakes, broke them into pieces with iron tongs, and filled the chillum. Then he came and sat at Zamir's feet.

'Zamir Mian, when are you leaving?'

'Tomorrow.'

Gandal was lost in thoughts. He puffed his chillum and said, 'Zamir Mian, if by chance you become a deputy there, send for Gandal to be with you.'

Zamir didn't reply. Gandal too didn't expect any. His eyes, though dreamy, had not closed. He said sadly, 'Chhote

Mian, my body does not have any strength left. See, my flesh now hangs loose from the bones. Abba Mian is no more, else I'd have got a pension…this body is of no use now, it's just a cage of brittle clay…a little more pressure and it'll crumble.' He grew quiet as his gaze shifted to the green fields in the west to watch the play of light and shade—sunlight racing ahead and shadows following. A thin layer of clouds spread over the fields. Beyond the sunlit fields, there was a group of bare-bodied urchins. Their faces were painted black and they carried small sticks which they banged on the ground as they sang loudly:

> *Black sticks, yellow sticks*
> *A cowrie shall get a good harvest*
> *Clouds will come, rains will fall*
> *A cowrie will turn into dust*
> *And water flow to the harvest.*

'There are clouds in the sky; it seems it will rain this time.' There was a mixture of hope and doubt in Gandal's voice.

Gandal kept gazing at the sky for a long time. He said sceptically, 'They are rising from the east. Who knows if they will bring rain?' Then he turned to watch Bunni and Achhe on the terrace of the new kothi.

'Butterfly, convey my salaam to Allah Mian!'

'And mine too,' Achhe added.

'Butterfly, butterfly, convey both salaams to Allah Mian!' As Bunni released the butterfly, it floated up toward the sky.

Gandal grumbled, 'These children create such a racket.' Then he shouted, 'Hey children, stay away from the parapet!'

Bunni and Achhe moved away from the parapet and disappeared. But soon after, two small heads peeped over the parapet again, before vanishing.

Gandal began to smoke his chillum. He kept gazing at the fields beyond. Then, as sleep seemed to overpower his entire being, he sang softly and sadly:

> *Hira, you wasted your nights in sleep, your days in eating.*
> *Your life was priceless, you exchanged it for nothing.*

Zamir sat, lost in his thoughts for a long time. He had left Badi Apa behind in the haveli. She was weeping. He had only caught a glimpse of Tahsina from a distance as the rooms were being vacated. She seemed sad and lost . . . He got up in a hurry and walked towards the kothi where the luggage was still being unloaded. The day was coming to an end and a lot of luggage had yet to be shifted. A row of carts continued to arrive. They creaked up, stopped, and offloaded their burden and went back noisily to bring back more luggage. Was it a haveli which was being vacated or a city? He became anxious. What would happen if everything did not arrive by the evening? He had to leave the next day. He began to think about his departure. For him, the haveli was like a fragrance from the past which had begun to fade like a dream. Now, his mind was focused on the journey ahead.

DASTAN

The Thunder of Rivers

Adalat Ali passed the huqqa to Hakim Ali, yawned, and said, 'Hakim Ji, the nights have become longer.'

Hakim Ji took a puff and replied, 'The nights will get longer now. The weather is changing.'

'Winter has almost arrived, Hakim Ji.'

'Yes, with the new moon, people will have to move their cots indoors to sleep. Already, the water feels cold when I wake up for my fajr prayers and perform wazu.'

Ghani interjected, 'Hakim Ji, it has been a long time since we heard a dastan from you.'

Siddique and Nasir agreed, 'Yes, Hakim Ji, it has been really long.'

Hakim Ji sighed and replied, 'Friends, I've now become a dastan myself.'

All of them fell silent. Adalat Ali spoke, 'Hakim Ji, when did we leave home?'

'Mian, a long time ago! Why recall those days? We left when the rains were almost over.'

'And when did the riots begin?' Ghani asked.

Adalat Ali replied, 'Mian, there were riots in June.'

Hakim Ji took a deep breath and said, 'Mian, I have no regrets except for the loss of the dastans I had collected—such dastans that made *Tilism-e-Hoshruba* seem like dust in comparison.'

Siddique once again insisted, 'Hakim Ji, it has been a long time since we heard a dastan.'

'Mian, all the dastans were left behind in Hindustan. Why? My entire library of dastans was looted; pages were torn and scattered; destroyed like the houses during the mutiny.'

Everyone fell silent after that. Hakim Ji continued to smoke the huqqa with his eyes shut. Then, he turned the nozzle towards Ghani and said, 'Friends, dastans were left behind in Hindustan—looted. Now only their memories linger. How can I tell a dastan when I don't remember any? I can recall only a piece here or a bit there, like a dream. I get lost in them. But, I can still recall one real dastan. Would you like to hear it? Mian Adalat Ali, do you remember the fakir who used to sit in front of my shop and shout: The waters of the Narmada roar, the streams of the Ganga roar?'

'Yes, yes, I remember.'

'He was not a fakir.'

'Really!'

'Yes. He was not a fakir. Friends, September is an agonising month. Two seasons meet like two eras and part. In that month, he used to suddenly go wild with frenzy and scream at night: The waters of the Narmada roar, the streams of the Ganga roar!

'I tried every possible treatment, but in vain. His condition did not improve. That incident made me lose faith in my ability to cure. When that fakir saw the state I was in, he laughed loudly in front of the patients sitting in my shop and mocked: O foolish hakim, O naïve doctor, whom are you trying to cure? I'm not mad, though madness is upon me. I was at first bemused, but later I began to pay attention to him. He sat down before me and told a dastan of such insight that everyone in the shop was in awe.'

Hakim Ji puffed his huqqa, cleared his throat, and resumed, 'Friends, listen carefully with your ears open and draw some lessons from it. This is a story of a bygone era, a dastan of lost cities—those streets and lanes have passed into lore now, their inhabitants have turned turn to dust. But if you think about it, you'll also recognise it as a tale of today; once again, our cities are being destroyed by the violence of the British and the changing colours of the sky. Our havelis are being reduced to rubble even now. The faith of the city is shaken once again and its people either lie buried or are homeless.

So friends, that fakir sat before me and, addressing all those present there, began his heart-rending dastan thus: Those who know, know; let those who don't know, know now that I am Samand Khan, son of Arjumand Khan, son of Rahavand Khan—a humble sepoy in the ferocious regiment of Salar-e-Azam, Bakht Khan. The British have tried their best to erase the name of that valiant lion and throw a veil of anonymity over his acts of valour. But can one hide the sun? The fame of his bravery still resonates from Hind to Syria and Rome. And, in every basti, his army passes through from Bareilly to Dilli, and men swear by his name. On winter nights, when bonfires are lit in village squares, dastans of his bravery ignite a flame in every heart and make the blood in every vein boil with anger; old grandmothers tell stories of his valiant deeds to children and young women sing songs for his return.

Friends, Dilli ruined us. All the paths from Bareilly to Dilli bear witness to why we rose like a raging storm in Bareilly and swept towards Dilli. Forests were devastated; mountains were crushed under the hoofs of our horses. Our army trampled across hills and deserts, dug up orchards, gardens, and fields, and broke over Dilli like a storm. But the lanes of Dilli were like the tangled tresses of a beloved. The Mughals betrayed my honourable master. Each morning, we buckled our swords for battle; but every evening, we put them aside. But that inauspicious city was marked for destruction. I clearly remember that every morning I used to hear a fakir sing from somewhere behind my tent:

> *Parrot, myna are nothing but dust.*
> *Cowrie, paisa are nothing but dust.*
> *King and subjects are nothing but dust.*

Dilawar Khan used to tremble with fear whenever he heard the fakir. Many a time, he drew his sword and ran out of the tent to behead him, but he never could find the fakir.

But something strange happened that morning. The fakir did not sing. The city was almost silent. We were getting armed for battle when Bakht Khan's voice startled us: Dilawar Khan!

Dilawar Khan reverentially walked towards him.

Bakht Khan showed him his ring.

Terrified, Dilawar Khan was speechless.

Friends, dear friends! You should know that Bakht Khan wore a ring with a precious turquoise stone. Many a battle he had won with its help. Every morning, as soon as he woke up, Bakht Khan always looked at that stone before he armed himself. That day, when he looked at his ring in the morning, the stone was cracked.

A little later, someone stood at the entrance of the tent. A chobedar, looking hassled and worried, entered and said: Huzoor, news has just arrived that the Emperor has deserted the fort.

Friends, the Mughals had betrayed my honourable master. I distinctly remember that day, as though it had happened yesterday. Bakht Khan was encamped at Emperor Humayun's tomb. We were standing in rows outside the tomb with our swords drawn, hoping that there would be a battle that morning, our wishes would be fulfilled, and those made of dust shall return to dust. Our battalion was smouldering with rage like a pan over fire, and every soldier was sizzling with anger like hot oil. Suddenly, Bakht Khan, seething with indignation, came out. His face was red with fury; he was sputtering with anger; he stomped the ground as he walked with such force that we were terrified and thought that the earth would crack and Humayun's tomb cave in.

But Dilli had yet to see some more battles, and Humayun's tomb was to stand witness to more horrors. Bakht Khan put his feet in the stirrup and mounted his horse. Then he turned to us and said: O illustrious companions! My loyal soldiers! We have been betrayed. Bravery and courage have departed from the house of Timur. The city has lost its sense of pride; its sense of honour has been erased. Now this city is doomed. Let us leave this city. It has led us to defeat; it has destroyed Bakht Khan; it has blemished the triumphant pride of Bakht Khan. The Shahjahani fort is shaken and is preparing for its ruin. The land of Shahjahan may not have us, but the land of Allah is wide open. Let us leave these vast plains. Let us move to the hills. Brave men fight in the plains, but meet a challenge in the hills.

My esteemed friends, if you can listen without losing control over your emotions, then listen to this exemplary tale. It was dusk when we left Dilli. After a day's journey, we were exhausted. The sun had set in the west and darkness spread over the waters of the Jamuna. Shadows crept over the parapets and towers of the Shahjahani fort. Far from the city walls, the ramparts, and the domes of the fort, we caught the last glint of sunlight over the tall Qutub Minar before it disappeared like a fading star. My honourable friends, darkness covered the battlements and fortifications of the city. The walls of the fort were silent like painted pictures. The canons on the turrets, which, till the other day, were booming and spitting fire on the enemy, were silent. We heard cannon fire from a distance—perhaps, the cannon at the Lahori Gate was still active.

By the time we left Dilli, it was night. The paths were lost in the darkness. Indeed, the darkness had so engulfed us that we could not even see our own hands. But the surge of Bakht Khan's regiment had broken all barriers. No one could hold back its onward march now. The torchbearers were ordered to come forward; torches were lit. The dark forest, the blazing flames of the torches, sparks emanating from the hoofs of galloping horses—our caravan blazed like Mars and rushed through the dense night. Tearing through the dark and cleaving the bosom of forests, Bakht Khan's regiment marched on under the veil of the night and covered a lot of distance. No one could tell what time it was, but the night was virtually past when Bakht Khan reined in his horse and asked: Friends, what place have we reached? Dumbstruck, we too reined in our horses and looked at each other, for none of us knew our location or had a clue about whether we were marching along a straight path or had strayed from it. Then, Bakht Khan said: O warriors! O brave-hearts! It is not wise to advance any further in this darkness without a plan. It is not prudent to risk our lives knowingly. We should now halt, rest a while, sleep, and think about where we are and in which direction we should proceed. Be thankful to the veil of the night that has hidden us from the eyes of our enemy. When morning comes and the news of our escape reaches our enemy, all hell will break loose.

At this, we dismounted from our horses and rested in that treacherous wilderness where nothing was visible except the tall, dark trees. What a wretched state we were in when we had set out from Dilli! We did not even have the bare minimum required for the journey. Samand Khan had never been unnerved in any war, no matter how fierce the fighting was. But tonight, after tying his horse to a tree, when he lay on the bare ground with his saddle under his head for a pillow, the naked sky above him for a roof, and infinite shadows of dark trees surrounding him, he found himself insignificant in comparison.

Beyond the wilderness of countless trees lay the vast sky where a procession of innumerable torchbearers, led by the planet Mars, was in progress. Suddenly, a star fell and a trail of light blazed across the sky, as though a well-built soldier had fallen from his horse in the battlefield, and, by and by, the news had spread. We had camped in the dark forest, but the procession of stars in the sky continued. At that moment, I felt as if an army of stars was passing by and the field of the sky was about to become clear once again. Who knows why, my heart began to beat faster at that thought and I closed my eyes. As soon as I closed my eyes, I was overpowered by sleep and all the frightening trees in the forest and the infinite stars in the sky slowly turned into dust.

When the morning star rose in the sky, we decided to march on. I went to wake up Bakht Khan, but he was already dressed. He looked disturbed. Dilawar Khan stepped up and asked: My honourable master! Why do you look so troubled today?

He answered: Dilawar Khan, I once had a strange dream which did not let me sleep. It troubled me again last night.

When we heard this, we became anxious and asked: O master, blessed with God's grace! What was that dream which has made our master restless and us anxious?

Bakht Khan replied thus: O my dear friends, my loyal companions! The dream was something like this: I saw Bakht Khan alone in a vast desert; separated from his army; his soldiers left behind. Then, I saw a tower blazing like a pile of burning embers. Its plinth was like a whirling millstone. I could not look at the tower, for all I saw were flames swirling up from the bosom of the earth and rising to the spherical sky. At first, I was scared and thought, Oh God! What workshop of dreams is this! But the very next moment, I said to myself, fear is against the code of chivalry. I shouted: Ya Ali! Then, I spurred my horse forward and rode slowly towards the tower. Strangely, the spinning wheel stopped. What unfolded before me now was a completely different scene—I saw a huge and wide millstone; and, standing on top of the millstone, I saw a tower made entirely of red stone. There was a dome on top of the tower with a huge drum in it. Beside the drum lay a spear. O, my dear friends, my loyal companions! At that point an idea crossed my mind. I decided to climb up to that dome, beat the drum, and witness the spectacle of God's miracles. The sound of the drum from that height would resonate far and wide and reach the heavens. When it falls on the ears of Bakht Khan's soldiers wandering in the jungles and the bastis without their companions, they would turn in the direction of the sound. Just as I decided to act, a voice rose from the tower: O fool, have some mercy on your youth! Stay away from this fiery tower. This is a perilous game of life and death. In this game, you must risk your life; your very existence may be erased! I took those words as a challenge. It was degrading and against my code of chivalry to retrace my steps. I said to myself: all living things are inferior to the son of Adam. Reckless and arrogant, I entered the tower. That tower, which glowed like an ember outside, was dark, dreary, and hot inside. There were winding stairs, which became even more forbidding as the millstone on the plinth began to spin as soon as I stepped on it. My friends, at that moment, I became aware of my frailty. I began to cry inconsolably. What a turn of fortune!

Bakht Khan, who always thought he was the bravest of all, who could challenge the mightiest and the most valiant of men in war, was being ground in the mill of time; and, even though he was a soldier, he risked being killed without a fight and without a purpose. Suddenly, what did I see! The entire desert began to reverberate with the sound of a galloping horse. A rider, dressed in green, with a sheathed sword hanging from his waist, rode into the tower. His face was covered with a veil. As soon as he stepped inside, the tower stopped spinning, the staircase became visible, and I woke up from my sleep.

Then Bakht Khan fell silent. The soldiers were engulfed by doubt and anxiety. I suddenly remembered the words of my ancestors and I respectfully submitted: O my worthy master, forgive my impudence! It was not a dream; it was a revelation.

Bakht Khan raised his head with great dignity, looked at me, and asked: Why?

The Story of the Shershahi Tower

I sat there respectfully and said: O, gracious master! I am Samand Khan, son of Arjumand Khan, son of Rahavand Khan, and I come from a very exalted family whose lineage goes back to Shershah Suri. I heard from my grandfather, who had heard it from his grandfather, that our ancestor Hazrat Shershah Suri had hammered a tower like a nail in the bosom of the earth. This was his last victory on earth. O, my gracious master, and O, companion of my actions! The conqueror of the earth, Hazrat Shershah Suri, treated this earth like a ball—he played with it, threw it up in the air, and caught it as he willed. He mapped and measured the entire land of Hind and linked it with roads in such a way that till today Calcutta and Peshawar are connected by a single road. It is said that once, as the army of Shershah was passing through the centre of the earth, and distances were reduced to dust, the earth reverberated with the thunder of galloping horses, which even reached the ears of the cow that holds up the earth on its horns. Suddenly, a vision of a fearful desert arose before the army. The sand was burning red and the surface of the earth throbbed like a heart. The horses stopped. The riders were alarmed. Hazrat Shershah tried hard to spur his horse forward, but the horse, which treated the spheres of the universe like dust under its hoofs, refused to budge. The sagacious vizier nervously advised: Jahanpanah, steer clear of this perilous route and take some other path! Hazrat Shershah became furious and answered: It is not worthy of a brave warrior to retrace his steps; it is not becoming of fearless conquerors of the earth to be awed by treacherous paths. It is against the nature of our horse to retreat as it just did. Surely, there is some mystery behind this. The code of chivalry demands that the knot of this mystery be disentangled and the truth about this spot on the earth be revealed.

So, the army of Shershah camped in that fearful desert and made every effort to discover its. The soldiers tried for two days, but could not find a clue to its mystery. On the third day, his majesty decided to solve the mystery himself. He mounted his horse, which had subdued the entire earth, and swore: Come what may, I will surely conquer the desert today.

He was about to spur his horse forward, when an elderly man appeared from nowhere, caught hold of the reins of the horse, and said: Oh Shershah, refrain from your plan! Have some mercy on your subjects! All the kings who have entered this desert in the past have lost their empires; their subjects have been exposed to misery; their wealth and country has been ruined.

Shershah asked: What was the reason for that calamity?

That wise man replied: O, subjugator of regions! O, conqueror of the world, this place is the centre of the earth. It is right in the middle of the two horns of the cow that supports the earth. This heart of the earth is an area of woe and suffering. It challenges those who play with danger and defeats them. The fame of the warrior, who subdues this piece of the earth and holds it in his fist, will spread far and wide, and his empire will expand from the Himalayas to Vindhyachal and from there to Raskumari.

Provoked, my forefather thought, now that I have set out on the conquest of the world, why falter, why withdraw midway? He invoked the blessing of Butarab and flung his spear with such force that it hit the centre of that desert. As a result, and quite mysteriously, the tremor in the desert stopped. My forefather then commanded: Let us commemorate our victory! Build a tall tower with a dome at the centre of the desert! Place a big drum in that dome! Whenever the drum is struck, its sound shall resound throughout the world, announcing the victory of Shershah!

Renowned and skilled architects were summoned from far and wide to design the tower. The tower, with seven floors and seven stairs, rose up to the sky. A dome was built above the seventh floor and a drum with a stick was placed in it. Then began a long wait for the auspicious time when the drum would announce Shershah's might. While we waited, something else was unfolding on the other side. Suddenly, a cloud of dust rose from the west and we heard the sound of galloping horses. When the dust settled a little, we saw waves of Rajput soldiers surging towards us, ready to take us by surprise. Shershah's army braced itself at once and broke like a calamity over the raging tempest of Rajput soldiers and chased the enemy away. But alas, while chasing the enemy, Shershah's army strayed so far afield that it lost sight of the tower. Then the rival army regrouped, restored order, and a ferocious battle followed. But the tower was lost from sight and the sun of Shershah's life was ready to set.

I heard it from my forefather, who heard it from his forefather that, as our venerable ancestor, Hazrat Shershah, lay dying, he informed his followers that when the sound of the drum from the Shershahi tower fell on their ears, they should know that the one who will fulfil Shershah's aspirations had been born. They should go and join his army. O, gracious master! O, companions in my quest! The vision of that tower in your dream indicates that we shall soon hear the sound of the Shershahi drum.

When Bakht Khan heard the interpretation of his dream, he asked: My friend, in which direction lies that tower and how many days will it take to reach it?

I humbly answered: O, gracious master, I have heard it from my forefather who heard it from his forefather that in the north-west, about a year's journey ahead, there is a dense forest. Beyond that dense forest, there is a black river, and beyond that black river there is a thorny desert. The sky-high tower stands in that desert.

Upon hearing what this humble soul had said, Bakht Khan turned to his soldiers and proclaimed: O, my illustrious companions, my loyal warriors! Surely, Shershah made the land yield to his design; he tamed the wild distances; but he failed to contain the river of time. Without time, this globe is nothing but dry grass. Time abandoned Shershah and reclaimed the earth from his clutches. The heart of the earth once again throbs as it used to, and the Shershahi tower spins like a millstone. The Grand Trunk Road he built groans under the feet of the British army. Dalhousie's steam trains run on its wounds. The sarais built by Shershah are deserted, the water tanks are dry, and the wells are either polluted or covered with dust or are filled with corpses. The trees lining the Grand Trunk Road no longer cast any shade or provide shelter to travellers. They now stand witness to the humiliation of princesses with delicate bodies, as they are unveiled, bound, and dragged in heavy iron chains. They see the horror and sing dirges to the grandeur of those who planted the trees. Friends, the cruel twists and turns of time betrayed Shershah. The rows and rows of prisoners on Shershahi roads call out to the heirs of Shershah. My soldiers! Listen to their voices, cut those barbed wires, and return the greenery and the shade to those trees. Today we survive to fight; fame and honour are our destiny; our fight is against time. Retreat would bring disgrace; turn back the tide of time! Stop the spinning of Shershah's tower! Let the drum be struck; let Shershah's name resound in all the four corners of the universe! Take hold of the reins of your horses and cover the distance of a year in a few months! This is your first battle against those who have subjugated the earth and conquered the world!

Then, Bakht Khan, burning with rage, mounted his horse, which was as powerful as the sea, and rode like the wind. I felt as though a fierce storm had risen in the sky. The gathered soldiers also mounted their horses. The earth shook, the forests were ruined, and the deserts trampled. It was as though an earthquake had struck. The earth was split into two. Friends, what a strange journey it was! The body of our horses defined the circumference of our existence. The rhythms of day and night collapsed. The line between morning and evening was erased. The division of minutes and seconds was obliterated. How could they stand against the flow of time! We were only aware of our horses and our bodies.

As we rode, we came to a dense forest. The moment we rode into the forest, it became dark. We saw strange birds and animals. Their cries were so terrifying that the bravest of our warriors turned pale, and the most lion-hearted of our soldiers lost courage. At that moment, Bakht Khan's imposing voice resonated through the army: Warriors, today we live to fight; holding back would be a disgrace. Our battle is with time. Retreat would be shameful.

Hearing these words, the soldiers gathered courage; the horses charged forward once again with such speed that all those uncanny noises were reduced to dust under the sound of the galloping hoofs.

The Story of the Dark River

Somehow, we managed to cross that dense forest. But it was still pitch-dark. The dark river was flowing swiftly. Its waves rose like glittering swords and dazzling daggers in the dark night; and friends, the sound of its roaring waters was eerie! Let it be known that it had rained heavily that year. All the rivers of Hind were inundated. When we crossed Ghaziabad at night, we heard a strange chant from somewhere far away: The waters of the Narmada roar, the streams of the Ganga roar.

Bakht Khan asked: Friends, what strange chant is that which makes our hearts beat faster and the blood in our veins freeze? Is it a celestial announcement or the news of a disaster?

A soldier from Meerut replied thus: Master, it is neither a celestial announcement, nor news of a disaster. Alha-Udal is being sung in one of our bastis. Rains have continued late into the year. Janmashtami is over, but the season of rain has not come to an end. The congregations are still singing the Alha-Udal.

Friends, the rains had really lasted for a long time that year. It was a season of heavy showers. All the rivers were flooded, and the lakes and ponds were overflowing like brimming bowls. We had left the Jamuna behind, as it crashed against the walls of the fort. The waves of the Ganga thundered from Hardwar to Calcutta. The waters of the Gomti burst its banks like the Euphrates; the Narmada was like Tatya Tope's army, which was, at times, fifty miles wide, and which, at other times, shrank and disappeared into the dark mountains. But the black river was the strangest of all rivers. No one could guess how wide or deep it was. All of us were awestruck. At times, the thunder of its waves sounded like the war cry of an army, at other times like a storm rising from the mountains. Friends, the sound of water had a strange impact. Warriors who were not deterred by the guns and cannons of the British stood paralysed by the roar of the waters. Suddenly, a horse neighed in terror, broke away, and rode off with its rider into the woods. While everyone was still in shock over what had happened and why, I noticed Dilawar Khan was standing next to me and trembling like a leaf and staring wide-eyed at the river. Even before I could bat an eyelid, Dilawar Khan screamed in terror, got off his horse, and jumped into the river. Dilawar Khan's leap into the river spelled calamity. The waves of the river thundered like clouds. Friends, clouds can thunder over the earth and lightning can strike under water. At that instant, clouds thundered over the river and lightning struck across its waters. It was as if the earth's crust had cracked and the molten magma was flowing out. We were hit by a storm so intense that the earth and the sky shook. Then, a rain of blood followed. Blood rained over the black river, the sky turned red like a new wound, and the forest blazed like red embers. Horses neighed in terror and soldiers lost hold of their reins and were thrown off their saddles; there was chaos everywhere.

In that commotion, my horse too went berserk. It screamed in fear and ran wildly. In the darkness, I could not tell where I was headed. I neither had my feet in the stirrup, nor the reins in my hand. When dawn broke, I found myself in a desolate place. There was no sign of a black river or a dense forest; nor was a soldier or a commander to be seen anywhere. There were no human beings as far as I could see. There was only silence. I remembered Allah and allowed the horse to follow its own instinct.

The Dastan of a Deserted City

As I rode along, I came to a basti. I thanked God and entered that basti, but it was a strange basti. There were neither beggars nor shopkeepers in it. All lanes and by-lanes were empty, and the houses vacant. Marks of gunshots were etched on the wall of every house. Havelis had caved in. Shops had collapsed. Signs of destruction marked every house; evidence of bloodshed was apparent in every lane. Market places and squares were strewn with corpses. The shops were unlocked and their goods were scattered all around. The doors of houses were broken and the gatekeepers had vanished. I was awestruck, and stood as if before a painted scene. Afraid and nervous, I rode into that city of the dead where I came face to face with a grand haveli. It had been smashed by cannon-fire. Several battlements had crumbled and lattice windows had been blown off, leaving large holes in its high walls. The haveli's gate was wide open. Its outer veranda was deserted, except for an elephant which had broken its chains and was roaming aimlessly, sniffing the moss-covered water that had settled around the fountain with its trunk. When I saw that frightening scene, a strange idea crossed my mind. I thought that if I went inside, I would be able to find a clue to the beginning and the end of this story.

When I stepped inside, I saw animals running wild. All hell seemed to have broken loose in the grilled coop of ducks; the hens shrieked in their enclosures. A big brown cat emerged from a room, looked wistfully at me, and began to meow. As soon as I opened the coop, the ducks quacked and the hens clucked as they ran frantically towards the moss-covered water around the fountain. Suddenly, countless beaks and claws were splashing in the water.

I saw a broad and spacious house as I stepped inside. It was built on a raised semi-circular platform. It had tall pillars and its high walls were in a dilapidated state. The large mirrors were cracked; the crystal chandeliers were all splintered; the candle-stands, flower-vases, incense-stick stands, rose-water bottles, lovely trays, delicate surahis, dazzling bowls, shining cups, heavy curtains with golden and silver fringes, and paintings of varied colours lay in chaos. It seemed as if a workshop of human craftsmanship lay scattered there, mourning its desecration and destruction.

When I came out of that grand hall, I found myself in a spacious courtyard. There was no one around. Its fountain was dry. Its marble basin was empty. Suddenly, a parrot shrieked and flapped its wings. When I looked up, I noticed a long and broad veranda in front of me. An elegant cage swung from a hook in the ceiling. In the cage, I saw a parrot with a red beak, a red ring encircling its neck and a red patch on its wings. It fluttered its wings and, with its beak wide open, screeched. I walked up to the cage and took it down. After a long search, I found some water for the parrot to drink. The parrot screamed: God is great. He is pure. Bibi is in the well.

The secret was thus revealed. There was a deep well behind the veranda. That is where the strange sounds were coming from. I untied my turban and dropped one end down into the well. Someone clutched it in the dark and I slowly pulled it up. When that soul came up to the edge of the well, a strange scene unfolded. It seemed as though a seed of light had sprouted from the dark, or a pearl had emerged from the gloom of a shell. Her body was iridescent, her cheeks radiated light like lamps, and her lips were like flames. But this light was dust-laden, her clothes were torn and dirty, and her hair was dishevelled. She was semiconscious. I immediately lifted that light-incarnate in my arms, laid her on the cot, and checked her pulse. Then I touched her cheeks and forehead to see if she had a fever. I sprinkled water on her face. I opened her lips and poured a little water into her mouth with my cupped hand. As soon as water touched her lips, she shivered, opened her eyes, and sat up. I heaved a sigh of relief.

For a long time, she sat like the epitome of sorrow in this woeful world without paying any attention to me. I could not gather enough courage to speak to her. Then, as she looked at her tattered clothes, she got up from the cot and walked towards the bathroom.

When she came out of the bathroom to dry her hair, I felt as though the monsoons had arrived and the sky had become overcast. Her body was like a luxuriant garden in bloom, her waist was sensual, her bosom like two lotuses with two tiny domes in the centre, her arms supple like boughs of a tree, her cheeks resplendent, her lips like budding flowers, and her eyes like jasmine! Flowers blossomed from my fingers and palms at the thought of having touched her a while ago. My imagination began to soar. She walked in gracefully and sat down on the cot. Finally, I enquired about her well-being. She replied: I am fine. The body aches a little. And I am angry. She sighed and became silent. After a while, she spoke again: My youthful friend, you have obliged me already. Now, have some mercy on your youth and leave this star-crossed basti. Who knows when the English soldiers will come back this way and kill all those who are still alive!

I controlled my tears and replied: I have been separated from my companions and have lost my way. Fed up with my life, I was wandering aimlessly in search of my friends when destiny brought me here. I consider your company recompense. But if you find my presence disagreeable, then this soldier, who has already lost hope and joy…

That beautiful woman became nervous and interrupted me: Oh no! You are a brave soldier. How can you shed tears over my insignificant words? This ill-fated one was only concerned about your own safety. But, already troubled, if you wish to add to your woes, you're most welcome.

Before she finished talking, my horse, tethered in the compound outside, neighed loudly. Alarmed by the thought that some more misfortune was upon us, I quickly grabbed that young woman's wrist and, dragging her away, said: The enemies have come. Let's get out of here.

Watching us leave, the parrot began to shriek. Hearing its cry, she turned around and said: I'll never go without my parrot. I grabbed the cage and dragged her out. I quickly jumped on my horse, pulled her up behind me, placed the cage in front of me, and spurred the horse forward. In a few seconds, the horse galloped away swifter than the wind.

Soon, it was night. A cool moonlight had spread all around, soothing the body. My thighs were glued to the saddle of my speeding horse, her heaving bosom was pressed against my back, and her arms were around my waist. My horse ran faster than the wind. I felt as if I was riding in the sky. That night was a reward for my skills as a horseman!

The horse's back was like the Garden of Eden in which, bathed in moonlight and drenched in dewdrops, we clung together as we flew like the wind. I felt as though my horse had covered the entire circumfrence of the earth.

The Story of a Jar and a Rider on a Cow

Late that night, we entered a basti. Enquiring around, we found a sarai. We rented a small and narrow room in which there was a cot and a soiled mattress. In such a grief-stricken time, we reckoned that even a corner was a blessing. I spread the mattress and then pulled out my sword and placed it between us. We lay there with our backs to each other.

But how could I sleep with the fire and excitement of the time we had spent together fleeing through the night? Besides, she was lying next to me and was yet so far. The night was spent uncomfortably. While I was still anxious and restless, I heard the same voice which we had once heard at dawn in that inauspicious city:

> *Parrot, myna are like dust*
> *Cowrie, paisa are like dust*
> *King and subjects are like dust.*

I was so tense and shaken that, in spite of all my efforts, I could not lie still. Restless, I got up and went out. The sky had brightened a little. The caravan of stars had passed by. The morning star was still shining, but the moonlight had faded. Suddenly, a rooster called and the sound of the azan rose from a distant mosque. After performing the wazu and other morning rites, I went into the small room and woke up that young woman. She hastily got up, adjusted her dupatta to cover her breasts and, rubbing her eyes, rose like a fragrance from the dirty mattress. She washed her face and hands, and performed her morning rituals. Then she took a turquoise-studded gold ring off her finger and gave it to me. She instructed me to go to the market, sell it, and arrange for food and lodging.

When I went to the market, I was confronted by a strange sight. The city had turned into a city of silence. The shops were open. People were buying and selling. But no one was talking to each other. People just bought what they needed and left quietly. No one laughed, joked, smiled, or gossiped. Intrigued, I roamed through the market the entire day and watched that strange scene. When it was evening, I noticed that all the inhabitants were walking out of the basti in large groups. They were quiet and sad. I resolved to find the secret behind the strange behaviour of God's people. So, I followed them.

Rows and rows of people were gathered in a large and open field. They were still and silent as in a painting. Suddenly, all eyes turned to look in the same direction. And guess what I saw? A fantastically dressed Englishman with a naked sword in one hand, foaming at his mouth, riding a cow, and shouting in rage! Two slaves, their faces veiled by long hair, stood behind him with drawn swords. They were followed by yet another slave who appeared to be from the hills; he was carrying a large jar on his shoulder. When that Englishman came closer, he jumped off the cow, sat cross-legged on a wooden cot, and placed his sword in front him. Then, he yelled at his slaves in an alien tongue. They rushed towards the crowd. The slave from the hills displayed the jar for everyone to see. The people watched in fear and revulsion. A young man in the crowd, his eyes blazing red with anger, shouted when he saw the jar. At this the Englishman once again thundered in his strange language, and the slaves, whose faces were veiled by long hair, pulled that young man out of the crowd, mercilessly chopped off his head and, leaving him to die, moved on to the next row. I was standing at the end of the row watching all this when the jar was placed before me. The entire scene was heartbreaking. The jar contained the severed head of a prince. His hair was black, his countenance was serene, and courage shimmered brightly on his face like the full moon on a dark night. My heart rose to my mouth and my eyes turned red with blood, but I considered it wiser to be patient and return home.

When I related the entire incident to that young woman, she clung to me hysterically, rested her head on my shoulder, and broke into tears. I tried to console and comfort her; I wiped her tears and reasoned with her. She continued to sob for a long time and then tearfully told me: My rescuer, the prince whose head you saw was my brother. This oppressed kingdom belongs to the king whose unfortunate daughter I am. My brother was killed in the battle. The British beheaded him and preserved his severed head in a jar. My father was captured. They hung him from a tree and burnt him alive.

When I heard this heart-rending tale, my eyes turned blood-red with anger. But Samand Khan was alone that day. What could he have done? I said: O sorrowful, grief-stricken princess, it is not safe for us to stay here. Let us leave this city and find refuge elsewhere.

The Story of a City without Street Lights

I quickly saddled my horse, seated her behind me, and rode away. Soon we were out of the city.

Overcoming all the obstacles and enduring the travails of the journey, we rode on. Soon, we passed through a town. We noticed something disturbing about the town and its people. The palace and the royal gardens were desolate. Decaying corpses lay strewn all around. Like the body of Imam-i-mazloom, the grand imambara was torn apart. The walls of the town were scarred by bullet holes, its towers had been destroyed by cannon fire, and its domes had collapsed. The townspeople were dressed in black. They were tight-lipped, silent and mourning, as if observing Muharram and reciting a marsiya. Even in the evening, when they left for their homes, they remained grim and sullen. The lanes and by-lanes were deserted once again. No shop was open; no lamp was lit in any house. The entire city was lost in darkness. Such were the days and nights in that city.

I spent the day watching that spectacle of mourning. When I could bear it no longer, I gathered courage and asked an elderly man dressed in black: My friend, what has happened here? The months of Muharram are over, but the town is still dressed in black and has yet not stopped mourning? I have heard a lot about how enthusiastically the people of this town observe the martyrdom of the Imam Shaheed, how they illuminate their azakhana with numerous lights, how their imambara dazzles with sparkling chandeliers, flickering candles and lamps; how the entire town glows with the glory of the imambaras; how sherbet is poured in the memory of Imam's thirst; and how sweetmeats are distributed, water kiosks organised, and majlis attended by the rich and the poor masses alike. But which season of mourning is this when the azakhanas are deserted, the lanes are dark, and the city seems to be so bleak and unwelcoming?

Tears welled up in the eyes of that elderly man in black when he heard me. He sighed and replied: My guest, my friend, this city is in ruins. How can the days of mourning end in the town when the taziyas have not yet been buried this year? How can people cast aside their clothes of mourning when they continue to mourn the exile of our king? How can the lamps be lit in the town when the light of our town, our queen, has left? As Mir Anis says: *Khursheed-i-darakhshan-i-imamat hai safar mein Gardish nazar ati hai us durr-i-qamar mein.* My friend, what times are you asking about? Neither the land nor the skies here are the same. The town squares have been destroyed, the streets are in ruins, the fountains of grace have dried up, and the clouds of tyranny have overshadowed us. The city is lost in darkness. The houses are desolate. Men from respectable families have been arrested and beheaded. O friend, what a season you have chosen to visit us! For our town, these are days of unhappiness and misery! What hospitality can we offer you? How can we play host to you? Our queen is in exile. The fragrance of our princesses fills the forests, while the town yearns for it. Oh, the hot days of summer and the difficult rocky terrains! Their fair bodies must have burned; their moonlike faces must have withered!

The elderly man sighed and fell silent. Then he whispered: My friend, our queen is observing the chilla ritual of Maula Mushkil Kusha in the hills. When that ritual is over, she will return and free our king; this town will then prosper once again.

After telling me all that, the elderly man quickly walked away, turned into a lane, and vanished.

I sighed in sorrow, returned to our sarai, and described all that I had witnessed to the young woman: Bibi, we escaped the town of death only to arrive in a town without lights. Those who live here weep for their prince and mourn for their lost homes.

When she heard about the town, she recalled her own and wept for a long time.

My honourable friends! Whenever that young woman wept, my heart melted, the heavy armour of soldierly life fell off, my entire being throbbed with pity, and the entire body seemed to melt like a soft, molten candle. That day, when she wept, I felt her sorrow more intensely than ever. Nevertheless, I did not consider it proper to express my feelings to the young woman. Instead, I explained to her: O young woman, it's our first night in this city. Your chastity is beyond doubt and your honour is unsullied. But this slave is just a human being and capable of immense evil. In fact, evil flows in the veins of human beings like blood. When the flesh awakens and passions beckon, what good is this unsheathed sword between us? How oft has one seen the barriers placed by custom and religion washed away in the whirlpool of passion? Oh, the agony of distance between bodies when our hearts desire union. When there is distance between us, then why are we so close? When we are so close then why this distance?

She blushed and was extremely embarrassed when she heard me. She didn't say anything. I cursed myself. A soldier that I was, I knew the tricks of the sword but was ignorant of the caprices of love. My efforts were wasted and I was hurt. While I was still lost in these thoughts, she passionately embraced me and began to weep inconsolably. I felt as though I was granted heaven. In her embrace, I thought I was strolling in the Garden of Eden. But suddenly, her mood changed. She said: My rescuer! What have you asked of me! You have put me on trial. My city has been widowed; the honour of my haveli has been desecrated. How can I adorn the nuptial chamber? I had vowed to serve the brave man who would avenge the murder of my father and brother and release my city from the clutches of the British.

When I heard her say that, my latent chivalry was awakened. I was reminded of my duty which I had forgotten for so long. I exclaimed: O gentle lady, you have opened my eyes. Bakht Khan had made Samand Khan promise that the sword raised against the tyranny of the British will not return to its scabbard. Only the bodies of the Englishmen will be its sheath. In the enchantment of love, I had forgotten his promise. You have reminded me of my vow. Now, I will set out in search of Bakht Khan, who must be in search of the

Shershahi tower. When the sound of the drum falls on your ears, know that the time to avenge your father and brother has arrived and that the tyranny of the British is over.

That was our last night together. We talked till late into the night about the impending parting and the joy of a future reunion. We did not realise when we dozed off. We had forgotten to place the sword between us. My mind was focused on the journey ahead. I woke up early. I felt as though the enchantment had broken; as though I had been thrown out of the Garden of Eden. Under the canopy of the stars, I saddled my horse. Then, I hugged the princess and set off on my horse.

By the time I left the city, it was already dawn. There were clouds in the sky. It had stopped raining and the sky was beginning to clear. At a distance, someone was shouting: The waters of the Narmada roar, the streams of the Ganga roar.

Soon, the monsoons set in once again. This was the first shower of the rainy season. Alha-Udal was being sung everywhere.

Samand Khan stopped after narrating his tale thus far, and fell silent. He sat there with his legs folded under him for a long time. He was still like a painted picture and his listeners were mystified. Then he said: Friends, Bakht Khan is still alive and searching for the Shershahi tower. When you hear the sound of a big drum being struck, you should know that it's time for Bakht Khan's armies to move and for Samand Khan to depart from your midst.

Then, Samand Khan quickly got up and left the shop, shouting: The waters of the Narmada roar, the streams of the Ganga roar.

We never saw Samand Khan again after that day.

Hakim Ji fell silent. Ghani, Siddique, Nasir, and Adalat Ali too said nothing.

Then Ghani nervously asked: Where did he go?

Allah knows! Hakim Ji answered: Only Allah knows where he went. He paused and then added: Many people were arrested in our lane that night. The kotwal came for me as well. But people in the city trusted me, so I was saved.

Adalat Ali quietly smoked his huqqa. Then he pushed its pipe towards Hakim Ji.

Ghani asked: Hakim Ji, is Bakht Khan really alive?

Hakim Ji, who was about to place the nozzle of the huqqa between his lips, dropped it and replied: That's what they say. Bakht Khan is still alive.

But how? Siddique asked sceptically.

Hakim Ji replied: This world is a workshop of wonders. Life is an enchanted story. No one knows the secrets of this workshop; no one can resolve the mystery of this enchantment. Death spares no one, and everyone who is born will die one day, but there are times when nature performs such miracles that life evades death. I've heard that when Bakht Khan set out from Dilli, the strange sound of a horse neighing fell on his ears as he passed through a village, but he did not pay attention to it and rode on. Later, a fakir met him on the way and chastised him: Bakht Khan, a curse be upon you! You did not pay attention to the neighing of Tipu Sultan's horse. The moment of your victory has therefore been deferred. Now the travails of time will chase you from desert to desert and you will waste away in the mountains. But you have escaped the cycle of life and death because you at least heard the neighing of the horse. When you hear that sound again, do not ignore it; follow it!

Ghani asked: Hakim Ji, what is the story of Tipu Sultan's horse? In which village did Bakht Khan hear it? Who was that fakir?

Hakim Ji replied: Friends, that is a long story and the night is short. The midnight bell has already rung. Sleep beckons. Let's call off this rendezvous for tonight. We shall end this tale tomorrow.

The Scream of the Horse

One day, the sun shone fiercely in the sky. The very next day, the clouds rolled up and it rained. Cots were once again moved indoors and people spent the nights of May wrapped in their blankets. This cursed weather was the consequence of the atom bomb, thought Nasir, but Ghani believed that seasons never remain the same in any country. If the normal cycle of seasons continues for centuries, one begins to feel that the cycle of seasons will never change, but it always does. To Adalat Ali, however, it was a sign of calamity: Can the dropping of an atom bomb disturb the cycle of winter, summer, and rain? I don't believe that.

Hakim Ji spoke up: Let's accept for a moment that the atom bomb has disrupted the cycle of seasons. But Bhai, what about the sky? You should take a look at the sky at night to see what chaos prevails there these days. Stars fall every now and then. Has someone dropped an atom bomb on the sky as well?

When they heard the news about a new comet, Hakim Ji saw it as an additional confirmation of his theory: Bhai,

Adalat Ali may or may not remember, but when I saw the sky in the winter of 1857, I had a premonition of an approaching calamity. The signs are not good once again. Last night, Mars was blazing like burning coal. Mian, I have grown so old, but I have never, in my entire life, seen Mars burn so brightly. In fact, looking at its rage, I thought it was going to challenge the sun. Now, tell me, has anyone dropped an atom bomb on Mars?

Hakim Ji's imagination ran wild. It broke the barriers of the here and now, and dwelt in some bygone era. Past incidents and memories, half-remembered dastans, forgotten people, he would catch one end of the thread and let the reel unwind on its own—there stands Tote Mian's father with a turban on his head and his gown on his shoulders, leaning on a stick in the middle of the courtyard, gazing at the stars. Tote Mian is sitting under the mango tree, feeding pieces of roti to the parrots or narrating his acts of valour to a rapt audience surrounding him. In Hakim Ji's mind, the thin line which separates a dastan from reality was almost obliterated. Countless people and incidents from his dastans seemed and felt real, while so many real incidents receded into fantasy. Hakim Ji always spoke of Tote Mian's father as if he had met him, though he had only heard about him from Tote Mian. Indeed, whenever he mentioned Tote Mian, he seemed to be narrating a dastan even though he had never seen him with his own eyes, walking and talking. Once upon a time, Tote Mian must have been a tall and handsome man; though now, he was no more than a handful of bones strung together. Time had deformed his face, though his eyes glowed as before. Lean and thin like a stick, his pale white skin was wrinkled. He had large eyes, and his long white hair, cut like an Arab's, was covered with dirt most of the time. He lived, if one can call it that, in a small room in Karbala at the edge of the town. Actually, he spent most of his time either under the mango tree opposite his room gazing at the stars at night or roaming all day shooing the parrots away from the mango grove in Karbala when the trees were laden with fruits. Flocks of parrots would rise together from the dense green leaves of the mango trees and descend on the tree under which Tote Mian rested. No one dared to shoo them away from that tree. The residents of the basti brought Tote Mian a lot of food, but he ate very little of it. Some of the food went to the destitute in the vicinity of Karbala, a small portion went into the stomach of those monkeys who hung from Karbala's dilapidated, grime-blackened domes, and a few morsels went into the belly of the dog that barked in the vicinity of Karbala at night and disturbed Tote Mian's reveries. The rest of the food was left for the parrots of the forest. Tote Mian set aside a few rotis from his dinner. At daybreak, when the morning star rose in the sky, he shredded the rotis into tiny pieces and continued doing that till the darkness began to fade from the sky, a faint white cloud of dust formed a halo over the trees, and parrots flying in from far and wide began to hover around Tote Mian. The screeching parrots landed near Tote Mian who stood in the centre and promptly scattered pieces of rotis for them. At times, a parrot got restless, broke away from its flock, flew up to Tote Mian, and perched on his shoulder, its long tail caressing Tote Mian's ears. But finding nothing there, it would fly back to the ground to join its flock. The entire scene rose before Hakim Ji's eyes. He clearly remembered those days in the past, those trees and the birds dwelling in those trees. Recalling Tote Mian, Hakim Ji lamented: Mian, those days are gone. Where do those things happen now? Then, he added gloomily: Such people, such affections cannot be found anymore. Men are now strangers to each other; what relation can they have with the poor birds!

He was quiet for some time and then resumed with a sigh: People are now so selfish they do not even offer a drop of water to the dying or lend a shoulder to the dead. Hakim Ji again sighed and became silent, this time for quite a while. Later, he wandered off into a distant world. He remembered how Tote Mian asked about the welfare of beggars in the neighbourhood of Karbala, or looked after them during their illness, or walked from tree to tree checking on parrots. Then, a strange scene rose before his eyes. Once it so happened that when Tote Mian began his daily routine of feeding bits of rotis to parrots, he noticed that the parrot that had dwelt in the hollow of the tree under which Tote Mian rested was lying dead as a log. Tote Mian was stunned. He remained very depressed and kept very busy that day. He went to the city early in the morning. People were surprised to see him and wondered why he had left Karbala and come to the city. Tote Mian collected a donation of one or two annas from the people in the market to buy some cotton cloth and camphor. Then he returned and made arrangements for the bird's burial. It was buried under the mango tree. Tote Mian sat by the grave till late evening, reciting verses from the Holy Quran.

That day when I went to meet him, Hakim Ji said sadly: I found him very depressed. He was so out of sorts that my words made him even more edgy, and he began to narrate his own dastan. It was so sombre that even I was saddened by it. That was a difficult night for all of us.

Yes, Sahib, what a strange man he was! Adalat Ali affirmed. But, Bhai, these fakirs are enlightened men.

Hakim Ji pointed towards Nasir and Ghani: They will not make any head or tail of this story.

Adalat Ali replied: Hakim Ji, my experience is that all these dastans only seem real; no one can make any head or tail of them.

But when Ghani and Nasir insisted on the story, Hakim Ji collected his thoughts once again. He puffed on his huqqa and said: Let the teller of a tale accept the curse and the blessing. I am going to relate verbatim the story I heard from Tote Mian without adding a word of my own. The death of the parrot had made Tote Mian melancholic. Speaking of the transience of life and impermanence of the world, he began to narrate his own story.

The Dastan of Tote Mian

Friends, today I'm homeless. There was a time when I was an important figure in a certain city and a certain lane. I lived in luxury. My life was a bed of roses. The story of that city is worth listening to, for rarely has the sky ever witnessed such a garden in bloom on the canvas of the world. The paths of that city were fragrant, its neighbourhoods were prosperous, and its lanes and markets were well lit. The shops in its small market, which was the hub of pomp and show, overflowed with expensive and exotic goods. Money was in abundance and goods were cheap. Transactions of millions were carried out in seconds. The merchants were prosperous and the people spent money with an open heart. Those who were not wealthy were generous and kind in spirit. The Jamuna of beauty flowed alongside the Ganga of wealth. Early morning, while it was still dark, women who were as lovely as the moon, yawned, rubbed their eyes still heavy with sleep and sweet dreams, and walked languorously towards the bathing ghat. How majestic the river looked when youthful bodies, burnished by the golden morning light, slowly slipped into the water! It seemed as if golden stars were being scattered on molten silver. The roses of youth blossomed; pink cheeks displayed spring; they were like pitchers of fresh juices which thieves could only lust after, but never manage to steal. Those were the days of amity. Pickpockets, thieves, and dacoits had to lie low. Men of honour were respected.

I spent leisurely days in youthful intoxication. I flew pigeons—oh, such variety I had! When the flocks rose up and swooped across the sky, it seemed as if dark clouds had gathered. Sahib, I am not exaggerating, but on days when the sun was sharp and it was very hot, my mother used to say, Beta, set the pigeons free for a while. I would go and open the door of the clay coop made exclusively for my pigeons. Fluttering their wings, flocks of pigeons flew out like clouds and the entire courtyard of my house was overshadowed in no time. Likewise, if ever the wind was still, my respectable mother would say, Beta, the wind is still, why you don't set the pigeons free for a while? Sahib, the moment the pigeons flew out of the coop, the flapping of their wings created such a stir that our sweat-drenched bodies were comforted! But, alas, I was separated from my pigeons: Laqa, Lotan, Jogiya, Shirazi, Kalami, and Lalsari. I had to abandon the terrace which was teeming with pigeons of all varieties and breeds. Separated from the world I once knew and the canopy of the sky under which I wandered, I still longed for those high terraces and pined for that sky. It was the second of March. The caravan of winter was leaving. The days were as long as the nights. Friends, it spells calamity when seasons meet, and day and night are equal and unite. Have you ever wondered why the game of destruction and creation is performed side by side in the month of March? There is such strange magic when two seasons meet—the wedding party of spring arrives on one tree, its branches are adorned with jewel-like flowers, and its leaves blow trumpets of joy. But the tree right next to it is without fruit, flowers, or leaves. Its bare branches look forlornly at the sky; a few yellow leaves, still cling tenaciously to their basti of branches, mournfully recalling old friends who left in winter's caravans; and when these leaves finally fall to the ground, they suffer the agony of any exile. All they can then do is sing dirges before they are finally swept into a pile in some corner.

It was the month of March. Friends, winters hurt, but when winter departs, it hurts even more. Ah, how many tales do winters bring with them, and how many do they carry away! Basant had passed a long time back. Holica had been burnt only recently. And people had begun to pull their cots out from stuffy rooms into the verandas to sleep at night. A sweet fragrance of fresh flowers and the buzz of bees had begun to spread through the mango orchards.

That was the month of March, and the day was of Nauroz. The sun was going down. A wooden cot lay in the shade. The courtyard was swept clean, the cot was covered with a clean white sheet, and a white bolster lay on it. My father's fair face was radiant; he was wearing a white dress, a shawl over his shoulder, and a fez on his head. Sitting with his legs folded, he held an open almanac in his hand. He had placed a bowl filled to the brim with water in front of him. A large rose floated on the water. A cup with rose petals was placed on one side and a pen made of a porcupine's quill lay on a white ceramic plate on the other side. Next to it was a bone-china bowl with yellow saffron water. Beside the bowl were sheets of white paper kept in place under some large fruit. Let me tell you, my father was a renowned amil and had knowledge of astrology. Every year, on the day of Nauroz, he sat in the same posture, and when the auspicious moment of Nauroz arrived and the rose floating in the bowl began to move in circles, he sat with his legs folded under him and wrote with saffron ink on the white sheet of paper.

Yes. So the almanac was open in his hand. His face was marked with anxiety. As he read the almanac, he said: The colour of Nauroz this year is red. The lion-rider has come with a bare sword in his hand. Who knows why, but my heart began to beat loudly when I heard him. Then I busied myself with the usual distractions. I played Nauroz with a squirt-gun all day, splashing colours on whoever I encountered on the way and laughing afterwards. So I didn't hesitate to throw colour on her too...Friends, I forgot to mention that one Hakim Zamin Ali lived in the same mohalla in which my house was located. He was a fair-skinned and burly man who always wore muslin. Even in the chill of winters, one could see him in a sheer muslin kurta sitting in his shop and drinking ice-cold water from a clay pitcher. He had a daughter who was very pretty and cultured. Her name was Shahzadi Mahal because her fair frame was as lovely as a marble palace. Tall and slim with pink cheeks, sharp features, a broad forehead, large eyes, and thick hair, she always wore a white chikan dress except during Muharram and the month of mourning, when her black clothes highlighted the lustre of her moonlike face. We grew up playing together, so there was no barrier of a veil between us, nor any restriction. We were not conscious of the attraction between us, but when our hands touched each other by chance while playing hide-and-seek, our hearts yearned to touch each other again; and when we placed our hands together to see whose fingers were longer, we deliberately argued. But, what happened that day was not deliberately planned. I unselfconsciously splashed her with colour from my rusted squirt gun. When that fair face was smeared with colour and her wet white dress clung to her shoulders and breasts, exposing her fair skin underneath, my heart stopped and I wished that a fountain of colour would continue to fall forever and the earth and the sky would dissolve in it. But my joy was brief, for I suddenly noticed that my honourable father, who had raised his head to stare at me, turned to his almanac once again without uttering a word. My hands froze; my heart sank.

That beautiful woman was forbidden to enter my house after that day. Her absence began to plague my heart. I could not concentrate on anything. All day long I sat on the terrace flying pigeons, and my eyes followed them longingly in the sky. But the sky too began to lose patience…Friends, during those days, the sky too had watched the earth and was mindful of its moods and fortune. It changed myriad colours, and countless stars fell from the sky all through the night like cannon shots. It seemed as though a war was being fought in the skies; that the stars would be extinguished and the bare skies in their wilderness would invoke the almighty. My mother was very anxious. Every time a star fell, she recited the *Lahaul*, shuddered, and cried nervously: Bibi, may Allah have mercy, something strange is about to happen!

My revered father would stand leaning on his walking stick in the middle of the courtyard and watch the sky for hours. It seemed as if he was either trying to count the falling stars or the ones left behind. Nervously, one day I enquired: Revered father, what kind of ritual do you perform when you stand without moving late into the night and gaze at the stars? What do you see there? What do the stars communicate to you?

Then, my father took a deep sigh and replied: My son, I read in the sky the future that is waiting to happen in the earth. The universe of stars is continually and eternally in motion. In the cycle of their movement lies the story of this earth and the universe. There are as many stars in the sky as there are pebbles on all the shores of this earth. They float in the sky like ships. But look at their order! They neither collide with each other, nor overtake one another. In the caravan of the galaxy, each traveller is alone. Without a companion or a torchbearer to show the way, bewildered and lost, each star drifts through the wilderness of the sky, traversing unknown and nameless paths. Countless travellers have lost their way in the desolation of the sky. But the trails they leave behind are never erased and their strong fragrance still lingers in the air. O, my dear son, the sky sparkles with the fragrance of those lost travellers and shows the path to those who travel on earth at night.

I understood and yet did not understand my father's words. But they reminded me of the star of my dreams who was no longer in sight, but whose fragrance floated on the horizon of my dreams making it sparkle. Hundreds of times, I would step into the lane and walk towards her house, but turn back in confusion; and then, on the pretext of flying pigeons, go up to the terrace and stare for hours at the terrace of her house and the staircase leading up to it. But the star of my fate did not rise. The stars in the sky fell as usual, and my revered father, leaning on his stick, continued to gaze at the sky night after night. This went on till September, the month of the union and separation of seasons. Friends, it was a September night. My revered father stood in the courtyard watching the stars late into the night. Then he went up to the terrace and, leaning on his stick against the highest parapet, gazed intently at the sky late into the night. There was a riot in the sky that night, and the stars looked like sugar crumbs. Then, a very big star fell and the entire city, dazzled by its light, woke up in alarm. My father hurried down from the terrace, mumbling slowly: *Wato izzo man tashao wato zillo man tasha* (You honour whom You please, and abase whom You please). Then he walked across the courtyard and shut himself in his small secluded room.

Friends, after that night, my father never came out of his small room. Day and night, he buried himself in the recitation of the Quran and prayers. His prayer mat was always spread, the Holy Quran was always open on its stand, a bare sword was always kept beside it, and his white beard was always drenched in tears.

One day, something strange happened. My mother became very restive early at dawn. She went and knocked on the door of my father's room. He unlatched the door and looked at my mother who was trembling like a leaf. Tears streaming down her eyes, she said: May Allah have mercy! I have had a haunting dream. In my dream, I saw a very large procession of men with uncovered heads and torn collars, carrying a lofty Alam in the front. Blood was dripping from the Alam.

My father did not interpret the dream and did not pass any injunctions. He took a deep sigh and intoned: *Wato izzo man tashao wato zillo man tasha.* And, then, he bent over the Quran once again.

My mother ordered a palanquin, left for the chhoti dargah, and there she clung to the zari and cried inconsolably for a long time. At dusk, when the lamps were lit in the dargah, she fell asleep. Suddenly, the entire dargah echoed with the sound of a galloping horse. The walls and the doors of the dargah seemed spellbound. By the time my mother woke up anxiously, the horse and the rider had disappeared. A large hoof-mark, glowing like sunlight, could be seen on the cemented floor of the Imambara. My mother kissed it. Then, she touched the patka of the bada Alam with her eyes and wailed profusely. By the time she returned home at night, she felt calmer and comforted.

Friends, now listen to this. On the third day, at dawn, my mother became restless once again as she heard the sound of a galloping horse. Anxious, she wondered if it was a revelation or a warning. She went and consulted my revered father. My father replied that it was a sign from God and men were not allowed to question it. Then he bowed down in reverence and my mother came out of his secluded room.

The city was in commotion that day. A strange rider, who was not visible to anyone, had entered the city. The few who heard the sound of the galloping horse thought that they had also heard a cry for help. They became possessed, picked up arms, and set out for battle. What a mysterious sound it was! Whoever heard it could not be restrained. Beat him, tie him with ropes, but he would break away, arm himself, mount his horse, and ride into battle. So, several young men of the city left their homes and rode into the battlefield.

When my mother heard the news, her anxiety increased. Then it so happened that after the gap of a night, she again woke up restless early in the morning and said to me: Beta, the horse rider is here again! She began to tremble like a leaf in fear and exclaimed: What a dazzling rider! Every wall and door trembles, and the sound of horse hoofs echoes through the lane.

I was strangely disturbed by her words and was anxious all day. By the time the evening lamps were lit, my fear intensified. Since I could no longer endure it, I presented myself before my revered father and respectfully pleaded with him: My wise father, may I die for you! Allow me to submit that my mother is in a wretched condition. The entire house is in grief. We haven't eaten a morsel of food. She is hysterical. Every now and then, she recalls the sound of a galloping horse. Father, what mystery of God is this?

What does the sound of the horse hoofs echoing in her ears signify? Do explain what she is saying to me.

The Story of a Horse without a Rider

My revered father thought for a while. Then he unsheathed his sword, placed it before him, and said: My son, the time has come when I should tell you the story of the horse rider and unravel the mystery of the galloping horse. My dear son, when the mission of the holy jihad was accomplished, and the enemy's sword had severed the pious head of Imam Husain, that faithful horse smeared its face in the holy blood of its enlightened rider, rode up to the entrance of the tent-house, and neighed sorrowfully. The princess of the universe rushed to the entrance of the tent in panic. When she saw the horse without its rider and its face smeared with blood, she untied her hair in grief and smashed her bangles. Then she remembered her husband's will. She wore a black robe, veiled her face, and, bemoaning the death of her husband, mounted the horse. The horse set off and disappeared into the forest. Writers have let loose the horses of their imagination and chroniclers have spilled a lot of ink, but till this day, the destination of that steed remains a mystery. O, my son, my life! How can the destination of that horse be traced; how can the inscriptions left by its hoofs be deciphered? Those forests were cut down; those fields were replaced by human habitations; and those hoof-marks were erased. Why be surprised by these revolutionary changes? That is how the world goes. Forests are cut down and cities are built; cities are destroyed and forests grow again. Everyone mourns for cities which are now desolate; but, friends, take care to also recall those forests which were cut down to build cities. What happened to those tall trees? Each tree was a city, each leaf a neighbourhood, each bud a lane. Vanished! My dear son, my father who was a renowned amil of his time, who knew the manifest and the unmanifest world, informed me that far from our city, there is a dense forest. It is the habitat of rare species of animals and trees. As far as the eye can see, there are trees; each tree is distinct; each branch is a unique entity. But there is one that stands apart—a very tall mango tree. No one knows who planted it or who watered it. Even before the Grand Trunk Road was built and Shershah had ordered all the trees to be chopped down, it had stood in its place, witnessing the changing colours of the sky and the desolation of the earth. That tree strikes a balance between the past and the future and unites the North with the South.

In the annals of history, the chroniclers have described that when Haider Ali was exiled to the deserts of sorrow and affliction, stripped of his entourage of ministers and soldiers, he wandered on foot from forest to forest. One day, in his aimless journey, he happened to pass through an enchanting garden. In that garden, he saw a lovely fountain that mesmerised him. It was surrounded by green shrubs of varied hues. The garden had shady trees; a cool breeze flowed through it; and it was filled with the fragrance of flowers. Haider Ali, who was tired and had not eaten for days, thought that the water from the fountain was like elixir from the heaven and the fruit was from the Garden of Eden. He plucked a few raw and ripe fruits, drank water from the fountain, washed himself, and lay down to rest under the shade of a mango tree nearby. As he had not slept for many days, the moment he lay down, he fell asleep. It was a strange sleep which brought with it tidings of mysterious things to come. In his dream, Haider Ali saw a rider dressed in green with his face and body veiled, exuding splendour and majesty, calling: Haider Ali, wake up! The horse is ready. Haider Ali recited the *Naad-i-Ali* and quickly opened his eyes. He noticed a horse, bright as sunlight, quietly grazing on the green grass nearby. It was a tall, white horse with a long neck, round hoofs, the mane like a fairy's tresses, a colourful tail, powerful thighs, flaring nostrils, and skin glowing like sunshine. Haider Ali considered his dream a prophecy, walked towards the horse, and held it. Reciting the *Naad-i-Ali*, he mounted the horse without a saddle and gently stroked it. His caress worked like a whip; a shudder ran through the body of the horse and it galloped away, trampling the green grass and crushing the flowers.

They say that Haider Ali rode that horse all his life, winning battle after battle and founding a divinely ordained empire. At the time of his death, he instructed his son: My dear son, my time is up. I am departing now. This divinely ordained empire is now in your custody. Expand it. Unite the North and the South, Kanyakumari and the Himalayas. I have handed over the royal treasure to you and explained all the secrets of administration. Consider my horse as the most precious of all my treasures, the deepest of all its secrets, upon whom this divinely ordained empire rests. If the horse goes berserk, everything will be ruined and the empire will disintegrate. If it ever neighs on its own, know that some grave threat is looming over the kingdom. Recite the *Naad-i-*

Ali, mount the horse, and ride into battle. Inshallah, you will find companions in the battlefield and will return victorious.

Ever since then, Hazrat Tipu Sultan, the martyr, valued that mighty and loyal steed, regarded it as more precious than his life, and waged and won all his battles riding it. Something strange happened in the last battle of his life—a little lapse of memory cost him the battle. The legend goes that it was the time of dusk. Hot winds were blowing. The dastarkhwan was spread out under the shade of a dense mango tree. Son, Hazrat Tipu Sultan was very fond of mangoes, and the shade of mango trees was very dear to him. There were varieties of mango trees in his orchard. He had got the cuttings of mango trees of all varieties from across the country and had them planted there. It was the second of May. The mango harvest that year was poor. The mango trees, usually loaded with fruits, were almost bare because of recurrent dust storms. But this orchard still had branches heavy with the burden of raw mangoes. The dastarkhwan was spread out beneath one such branch. A wide variety of food of different colours was laid on it. The nobles and the men of the highest ranks in the administration sat there in rows. The Sultan sat in the middle. He was about to start eating, when the neighing of his faithful horse from a distant place fell on his ears. Hazrat paused, hesitated, and then decided to continue eating. While the food was still on his plate, a large leaf fell from the tree on his plate like a shield falling from the hands of a struggling soldier. The mighty leader stopped and looked up at the tree. While his gaze was still fixed on the tree, his faithful horse neighed again, this time with such force that the entire fort reverberated and the earth shook at the sound of a galloping horse. The master turned and saw that the horse had snapped its leash, escaped from the enclosure, and was charging in his direction. At the same time, he also saw a messenger running towards him from the battlefield. Harried and weary, the messenger came and announced: May the glory of the Sultan remain intact! His faithful general has been killed. The British forces have scaled the walls of the fort.

On hearing this, the mighty king seethed with rage. He got up and commanded: Saddle my horse. The time for me to go to the battlefield has arrived. Then he looked so sternly at the nobles that they turned pale with fear. Angry and agitated, he unsheathed his sword and broke the scabbard and mounted his horse. Strangely, in his wrath and frenzy, the Sultan forgot to recite the *Naad-i-Ali*. When he spurred his horse, it refused to budge. It struck the ground with its hoofs and did not move. The Sultan was confused and flustered. He gazed at the sky and then turned to his horse and said: My faithful steed, my companion, my friend, has your sense of loyalty vanished? This remark had its effect on the steed who scoured the ground with his hoofs and galloped off like an arrow towards the ramparts of the fort. But the loyalty of the steed could not make amends for the error. When the Sultan fell to the ground, he realised his mistake, but, by then, it was too late.

My son, the chroniclers have exercised their pen a great deal in describing the martyrdom of the Sultan, but when it comes to the description of his horse, they fall short. But who can rein the horses of imagination, and who can erase images etched on the mind and the heart? The legend that has passed down by word of mouth from generation to generation and rages in the heart like truth goes thus: When the Sultan achieved martyrdom, his loyal horse smeared its face in the Sultan's pious blood and left the battlefield. The horse was like the last ember from the battlefield; it ran towards the forest where it still burns like a bright flame.

The tragedy was that a perfidious minister saw the horse galloping out of the battlefield. Since he was familiar with the virtues of the horse, he rushed to inform his British masters that a calamity had happened. The Sultan's horse had escaped. Now the news of the Sultan's death would spread like fire all through the kingdom. Any brave young man who dared to mount the horse would become another Tipu Sultan. My dear son, this was the last conspiracy of that battle. I heard it from my father who had heard it from the chroniclers of his times that the loyal horse, after it escaped from the battlefield, was headed towards Khyber. Had it reached Khyber, there would have been mayhem from the North to the South and from the East to the West; but it was destined to be otherwise.

The British army gave chase to the galloping horse, raising dust over a long distance. The sound of running horses reverberated from the nadir of the earth to the zenith of the skies. In the chaos of the chase, lush green fields were crushed and several forests were trampled. Such was the magic of the majestic horse that at one moment it would display its elfin power and gallop away without even breaking an egg under its hoofs, and, at other moments, it would cause sparks in rocks and tumult in oceans as it ran past them.

Soon after the homeless and exiled horse had galloped past a particular basti and a particular place, it entered the forest and came to a special mango tree with dense leaves. So strange was the perfume from the mango tree that the horse stopped. My dear son, it is said that the tree under which Tipu Sultan had his last meal was grafted from that ancient tree. The steed paused under its shade. A British soldier, who was chasing the horse and was known for his marksmanship, shot the horse. When the enemy forces came closer, they saw fresh blood under the shade of the tree but not the horse. They searched the forest and the fields, but the horse was nowhere to be found. The horse has been missing ever since. Allah is omnipresent, omniscient, and this world is a workshop of miracles. Every creation on this earth is strange; every event extraordinary. That which we can see suddenly becomes invisible; reality transforms into fiction. My father has informed me that the same horse, like a restless soul, wanders in forests like a vagabond fragrance. It will pass through this city one day. The city will reverberate with the sound of its hoofs and there will be a big battle. Then, it will be doomsday.

My father fell silent. Lost in deep thoughts, I sat there for a long time resting my chin on my knees. Later, when I stirred, I asked: O, my revered father, you have narrated the story of Tipu Sultan, but you still haven't explained why that steed wanders through forests like fragrance. My father replied: O, my dear son, that horse is waiting for its rider. Only when the warrior who can ride it into a battlefield is born, will the soul of that pious horse find peace.

I asked: Father, how can one find the horse and what are the conditions for riding it?

My father answered: My son, I've heard from my father that only a warrior can find that ancient tree in the forest and see that horse saddled and neighing under its dense shade.

I again asked: How can one find that forest and how can one identify that tree?

He replied: Dear son, that forest is invisible to the human eye. Only the birds know its whereabouts. The birds perching on its branches are safe from all threats and dangers. The parrots with melodious voices, who are related to that ancient mango tree, first circle over it before they come to rest on any other tree. My father has informed me that the brave one who depends on his valour and follows the advice of the parrot will fulfil his mission. He will ride the horse, reach his destination, and emerge victorious.

Friends, this story had such an impact on me that sleep forsook me at night. I spent many nights in utter restlessness. Every time I dozed off, my sleep was disturbed. Whenever my eyes opened, I saw the lamp lit on the namaz chowki, the prayer book open in the front, and Ammi trembling like a leaf as she recited the *Munajat* in her doleful voice: *Ya Ali, ya Eilia, ya Bulhasan, ya Butarab*…And I always found my revered father standing in the courtyard, leaning on his stick, and gazing at the changing sky. Tonight, again he came out of his secluded room, and so poignant was the mournful voice of my mother reciting *Ya Ali, ya Eilia, ya Bulhasan, ya Butarab*…that my sleep was disturbed by it several times. After a while, the same voice lulled me to sleep. Around dawn, I felt someone shaking my shoulders. When I woke up, I found my father standing near me, shaking my shoulders, and saying: Wake up son, the morning star has risen. The call for prayer has begun.

I got up. I saw that my father had a white turban on his head, a shawl on his shoulders, and a green sash around his waist. He stepped forward and embraced me. Then he benevolently caressed my head. I realised that his body was trembling from top to toe and his tone was slightly mournful. He said: Son, I'm going to discharge my morning duties. Take care of the house.

I couldn't understand anything and watched him in shock. By the time I collected myself, he had left the house. The rattle of the door-latch opening and closing was lost in the sound of a horse galloping down the lane.

Bewildered, I got off my bed and walked towards my revered father's secluded room. I opened the door and noticed that the sword which used to lie unsheathed every night in front of my father was missing. I left the room and climbed straight up to the rooftop. The darkness of the sky had been washed away. The caravan of stars had dispersed except for a few vagabond stars which were still lingering in the sky. The high terraces, tall minarets, and domes were still steeped in darkness. Somewhere far from those terraces and minarets, cannons were thundering and the distant sky was red. In no time, the image of a horse without a rider rose before me and the sound of its hoofs began to rage in my veins like blood. My body was burning. I came down in a state of frenzy. I looked at my mother who was sleeping. The prayer mat was spread on the namaz chowki, but its corners were folded. The candle was extinguished. The courtyard was still drenched in darkness, though the upper walls and the edges of the parapets were bright with the morning light. The courtyard was silent. Only the sound of pigeons cooing in their coop floated up into the air. I looked anxiously at the courtyard, at the sound-filled pigeon coops, and at my sleeping mother before I quietly opened the door and walked out.

Friends, it was the month of March. As the month was coming to an end, the nights became shorter and the days grew longer. The branches of the mango trees were laden with fruits, and bees hovered over the sweet, ripe mangoes. It was early morning and a lone sparrow hopped freely over the mist-covered parapets. The morning breeze was blowing gently. The scent of ripe mangoes floated through the air. The shops were still shut and the sounds of daily routine had yet not filled the lanes.

I walked through the markets and lanes for a long time. The sun was now much above the horizon. The shutters of the shops were still down, the busy neighbourhoods lay silent, the roads were deserted, the windows were shut, and the doors locked. The chowk, which usually buzzed with activity from dawn to midnight, was deserted today. There was an eerie silence which had descended on the city. I was walking alone on the road and was alarmed at the sound of my own footsteps. Suddenly, at a distance, a green alam appeared. Its bright radiance dazzled my eyes. After a while, I paid attention to the man who was carrying the alam. I saw a well-built warrior mounted on a horse riding towards me. He held the alam in one hand and a spear in the other. There was a white turban on his head, a green shawl on his shoulder, and a black veil covered his face. Suddenly, the horse stopped. The horse rider raised his alam, shook his spear, and shouted so loudly that the walls shook: O men, who are gathered here, beware! A deluge is about to hit your city and will sweep away your houses, mosques, tombs, and dwellings with its force. O men, the houses of God have been desecrated; the dome of the sky has turned dark; the sun is smeared black; the days have turned dark like the nights. O men, life is cheap and death has become precious. Today, life is no more valuable than the sneeze of a goat, whereas death is sweeter than a mother's milk. O men, take heed, the time of your greatest trial has come! The battlefield beckons you; your horses are restless!

The speech had a strange impact. In no time, the deserted streets began to echo with the noise of footsteps and locked doors began to open one after the other. Valiant young men in white turbans, girdles, and unsheathed swords came charging out from every lane, either on foot or horseback. Soon, an entire rebel army was formed. Then that horseman pulled out his pearl-studded dagger, tossed it to me, and rode forward, urging the rebels to follow.

The green alam, the horseman, and the rebels vanished from sight and the markets were once again deserted. Confused and amazed, I wondered, O God, am I dreaming? Did I see an army just appear and disappear in an instant? But the moment I picked up the dagger, the blood in my veins began to roar and my ears rang with the neighing of that horse without its rider. I fastened that pearl-studded dagger in the sash around my waist and ran back to my house. My eyes were still dazzled by that dream; the blood in my veins still roared; and I could still hear the sound of galloping horses. I knew it was time for me to go home, seek permission, bid farewell, and ride into battle.

When I turned into my lane, I was startled by a strange sight. There were fresh hoof-marks everywhere, as though a rebel army had just passed through the lane. All the doors were broken, the screens were smashed, and the windows were blank! I was shocked! What could have caused this sudden havoc? Then, I heard the frenzied screech of a parrot. What I saw before me was the body of a handsome and gentle young man smeared in blood and dust. His lips were like the wilted petals of a rosebud; his fair and flowerlike face was crushed; his eyes were smudged with kohl; and his forehead, ringed by curly hair, was encrusted with dust. He wore a muslin kurta, revealing a delicate body. A terrified parrot, as if aware of the fate of his master, was screeching and desperately fluttering its wings in the cage clutched tightly in the young man's fist. Friends, the corpse of this handsome young man was the younger brother of the same beautiful girl who had once risen like a star in the horizon of my consciousness. I realised at once that some calamity had happened in their house. I unlocked the door of the cage and the parrot flew away. Then I ran towards the haveli. The courtyard was deserted, the gates were open, and the hakim's shop was shut. I couldn't make out anything and kept calling for a long time: Qibla Hakim Sahib! Qibla Hakim Sahib! But there was no reply. A pair of wild pigeons fluttered their wings as they came out from the lattices of the high roofs and flew away. The entire place was empty and deserted. When my voice echoed through that high-roofed house, it felt as though someone from another universe was responding to my call. My heart began to pound and I quietly slipped away and went back to my house.

When I got home, I found that it too was deserted. I looked into every room and called out many times, but there was no response. My father's room was shut and the prayer mat was spread over my mother's namaz chowki as usual. The sijdegaah was in its proper place and the prayer book was open, as though she was in the middle of reciting *Ya Aliya Eilia, ya Bulhasan, ya Butarab*, and had just gone out for a while. The house, the veranda, the rooms, and the courtyard were empty. However, chaos prevailed in the coops where the pigeons were kept. It was already afternoon and the pigeons had not been let out. I walked up and opened the doors. The pigeons flew out with the desperation of prisoners freed from their prison. I scattered seed for them, filled water in their bowls, threw a last glance at the courtyard swarming with pigeons, and left.

As soon as I stepped into the lane, the noise of galloping horses fell on my ears. I ran like an arrow to hide from them in the courtyard. A cavalry charged into our lane and after shouting incomprehensibly rode into the next. But when I came out of my hiding place, I was confronted by a rider who had lingered behind. I invoked the blessing of Maula Ali and flung my dagger at that rider. It hit him in the chest and he fell from his horse. I ran forward, pulled my dagger out of his chest, sheathed it, and, mounting the horse, sped away from the place.

Before leaving, I turned to look wistfully and for one last time at my lane, my house, and the haveli. Its tall doors seemed so forsaken. I only recall seeing a lone kansuri perched on the dome of the house. I rode out of my lane and turned into another. Soon that lane, those walls and doors, the tall gates, the elevated canopy over the terrace of my house, and the entire skyline disappeared from sight.

When I turned towards the main market, I came across a dog dozing in the middle of the lane. On hearing the sound of a galloping horse, it slowly opened its eyes, rose reluctantly, and walked leisurely away into another lane. A little further ahead, I saw some crows sitting on the road. When they saw the horse charging at them, they simply hopped aside to escape its hoofs, and once we rode past them, they moved back. I heard the sound of gunfire being exchanged somewhere nearby. Then, the sound of firing moved further away. Loud explosions were followed by utter silence. Suddenly, dust rose at the far end of the road and I caught the sound of a horse galloping towards me. Then, as the dust settled, I saw a rider charge in my direction. He whizzed past me like an arrow and the road was deserted once again. At times, the window of a house opened slightly; a pair of frightened eyes and an anxious face looked out from behind a curtain and vanished in a flash.

I rode through the main market and reached the chhoti dargah. I tied my horse outside the dargah, left my shoes on the steps, and walked in reverentially. As soon as I entered, my eyes fell upon the marble water tank in the middle of the courtyard. A benign and saintly soul, the epitome of fortitude and forbearance, was sitting by the side of the holy water tank and performing the wazu. Suddenly, the entire courtyard was filled with the clatter of a horse. Its rider was a tall young man with a broad chest. He held a sword in one hand. He leaned down, cupped some water in his other hand, and asked: Can I empty it? That pious old man looked at the youth serenely and answered: No. The rider in whose cupped hand water surged like an ocean quietly let the water fall back into the tank. Suddenly, there was a flash of bright light and the entire dargah reverberated with the thunder of galloping horses. I was blinded by the light. In the next instant, both the holy old man and the rider vanished. The water tank, made of white marble, seemed like an eye filled to the brim with tears.

My heart was filled with the sea of faith; my eyes were dazzled by the miracle they had seen. I came out, mounted my horse, and rode away. All the lanes and by-lanes were desolate, but the market was bustling with activity. There was, however, an extraordinary commotion in one lane. Many of its shops were already closed, while the doors of others were being locked. Expensive goods were tastefully arranged in them, but there were no sellers or buyers anywhere in sight. Pushcarts were being hurriedly rolled away, while hawkers were packing up quickly. The inhabitants had either locked themselves inside their houses or were running away from their homes, as if from an earthquake. Huge gates and high entrance doors were being opened or shut with a bang; and those who rode out on their horses to join the rebels with naked swords seemed determined to die. The rebels were a motley and colourful crowd. Some wore khods over their heads, some turbans; some wore topis, while others were bare-headed. Those with swords brandished them; those with spears shook them. There were many who had neither swords nor spears. Some of them had picked up splintered frames of cots, as if they were deadly weapons; others had grabbed planks of wood. Some came out carrying gunny sacks overflowing with grain. The rebel army, free from all restraint, swelled like an ocean and was filled with pride. Suddenly, I caught sight of the same alam with a green flag fluttering at the top. The rider stood up on the back of his horse and exhorted the rebels loudly: O men, beware! A calamity is about to fall upon you. The battlefield is calling out; your horses are raring to go; their backs are desperate for their riders.

Upon hearing these words, the raging army of the rebels began to brim with wrath and, roaring like a deluge, moved on. I urged my horse forward and joined their noisy ranks. Wide-eyed with wonder, I looked around as a veil of dust was raised by the galloping horses. I was surprised when I realised that the horseman dressed in green had vanished from sight. When I looked again, I noticed that the battlefield lay ahead of me. There was a loud beating of drums. The sound of trumpets splintered the sky. The roll of drums, the noise of cymbals, the lament of tambourines—the battlefield shook as warriors, with the courage of lions, charged forward on their horses and challenged their enemies. Arab, Turkish, Iraqi, Bahmani, Kathiawadi, Deccani—horses of all breeds with broad chests, translucent skin, and long necks were gathered there. Cannons were placed on the backs of the finest elephants whose trunks and tails were raised in fury. When the cannons were fired, they seemed to rent the sky. There was one elephant in particular which was ornately decorated; its trunk was painted, its forehead had floral designs, its back was covered with fine golden cloth, its tassels were woven from threads of gold, its chains were long, and its canopied howdah was made of silver. A majestic princess, whose radiance lit up the gloomy desert, sat in the silver howdah. Indeed, it seemed as if a carpet of stars was spread on the earth. Fragrance from her body wafted through the battlefield. In her lap, she carried a parrot in a cage. Like stars encircling the moon, she was surrounded by fair maidens who fanned and caressed her with peacock feathers. Some of them sprinkled rose water on wounded soldiers. The water carriers went from soldier to soldier to quench their thirst and wash their wounds.

My gaze was transfixed on that one luminous face among those on the howdah, and I thought of Shahzad Mahal. Suddenly, I was tossed aside by an elephant. Dust and smoke obscured everything. The elephant went berserk. The battle-lines were confused. In no time, the exalted soul sitting on the elephant along with her attendants was surrounded by her enemies. I unsheathed my sword and charged towards the elephant. A few other brave warriors joined me. The battle was so fierce that both the armies seemed caught in a whirlpool. Their ranks and files fell over each other like chaotic tides. Rivers of blood began to flow. We didn't let the enemy come anywhere near the revered howdah. We rescued the princess and her companions from the battlefield with such care that the fans made of peacock feathers held in the fair hands of maids never stopped moving; the bottles of perfume did not shatter; the paandan remained open; and the silver bowl in the hand of the Janab-i-Aalia, brimming with the sherbet of saffron, did not spill on her beautiful garment.

On the battlefield, who cares about one's own fate? But later, when I looked at myself, I saw that I was severely wounded and bleeding profusely. Weakness overpowered me. My feet felt limp in the stirrups. I could not hold on to the reins any longer. In a delirious state, I felt as though someone was supporting me. Then, slowly, everything around me grew hazy and a thin mist of oblivion fell over my senses.

I don't know for how long I lay in a stupor. When I regained consciousness, it was already dark. The wax candles in the glittering candle-stands were lit. Amber and incense sticks sparkled in holders made of gold and silver as blue lines of smoke curled up from them. Someone made me inhale from the censer, and someone else sprinkled rose water on my face. Aromas of all kinds filled my brain and body. But more powerful than all these was the perfume that rose from the body on whose velvety bosom my head was resting. Her long tender fingers caressed my forehead and slipped through my hair. Such was the impact of her touch that no sooner had I regained consciousness than a film of drowsiness covered my senses. My wounded body felt soothed. I desired nothing more than to lie on that soft bosom forever. A sweet languor flowed through my entire being and overpowered all my senses. Suddenly, she called her servant and, in my nervousness, I opened my eyes. I saw Shahzad Mahal fanning me with her henna-coloured hands and sprinkling rose water on my body. Apprehensive, I tried to get up, but she gently held my head and placed it back on her bosom. Our eyes met. Besides the joy of the unexpected reunion, I was perplexed. She did not answer my question, but her eyes welled up. I could not bear to see her tears. I shut my eyes. All kinds of fear and doubt plagued my mind.

Your revered father...she stopped. Her voice choked even before she could speak. She paused, composed herself, and resumed: Your revered father left for his morning prayers, never to return home. That morning, many devotees did not return after the namaz. What terrible news and ominous messages kept pouring in! Some said that the minarets of the mosque had fallen and its courtyard was inundated with the blood of devotees. There was a rumour that the devotees had followed a horseman wearing a green robe. Such words of ill-omen were uttered that mishaps began to happen. Cannons began to spit fire and raze buildings behind our lane. Baba Jaan hurriedly gathered his family together and went to your house to persuade Khala Hazrat to escape with us, leaving the haveli unguarded. In our hurry to leave, we left everything behind. Of course, Tafan Mian took the cage of the parrot with him. She broke down, paused, and then resumed: Our lives were all that we could take with us, but we couldn't keep them safe. A despicable British regiment charged into our lane. Their guns scattered us like roasted gram in a clay oven. I was the only unlucky one. I was so scared that I ran away from there. I was not conscious of my body or clothes; trying to escape, I even lost my chadar. My share of misfortunes was yet not over. A royal servant, who used to visit my father daily to inform him about Janab-i-Aalia's condition and collect her medicine from him, came that day too. He was shocked and deeply distressed when he saw my state. He took me to Janab-i-Aalia and, throwing his turban on the ground before her, declared: O Janab-i-Aalia, may I sacrifice my life at your feet? The wise hakim, the pride of physicians, the Galen of our times, has departed from this world. He has attained martyrdom. His unfortunate daughter, unveiled and uncovered, has become homeless. She has escaped the siege of enemies. This humble servant of your palace found her distraught and unveiled. I have respectfully brought her here and present her before you.

On hearing this, Janab-i-Aalia grew sad. Affectionately, she looked at this humble soul, gently placed her hand on my head, and took me in as a maid under her care.

After narrating her story, she became silent. Her voice was tearful. Still lying with my eyes closed against her bosom, I felt a tremor run through her body. Then, a warm tear fell on my forehead. I did not have the heart to open my eyes. So I lay silently with my eyes closed, while that beautiful body continued to tremble.

In the morning, I noticed that my shoes lay on top of each other. That was a bad omen and made me afraid of what further calamities my wretched fate had in store for me. Through which forests and countries was it going to take me now? In the meantime, Shahzad Mahal nervously exclaimed: Ya Ilahi, have mercy! Why is my left eye twitching?

We looked at each other and saw doubt and anxiety in each other's eyes. In some inner recesses of our minds, unknown and strange fears lurked.

When we looked around, there was gloom and sorrow everywhere. The royal servants were mourning quietly. The maids were sad, silent, and cheerless. Some seemed lost in the thought of a bygone era, some gentle souls were stunned into silence, some sat silently with their heads down, some sighed, and some had tears streaming down their faces. Upon enquiry, we discovered that the Janab-i-Aalia had seen the exalted Sultan in her dreams. Since then, the image of the Sultan's face had hovered before her eyes and his memory had tormented her. Her servants were concerned about her condition and remembered the exalted Sultan.

It was only after the Janab-i-Aalia forsook food and laughter in the memory of the Sultan that the parrot began to speak: Allah Almighty is Truth, Allah is right. Right is His Prophet. Don't be oblivious of Him. Don't forget Him. Live long and keep invoking the name of the Prophet. Get up, Fakir! Let's go to Mecca.

Then the Begum's parrot continued thus: In the East, more than a year's journey from here, there is a dense forest. Beyond the forest is a river. Beyond the river lies a sea. On the shore of the sea, there is a harbour. There is a British encampment at the harbour. The enemy holds sway over it. The fortress at the centre of the city is made of baked clay. In that fortress, there is a garden. And in that garden, there is a cypress tree. On that tree, there is an iron cage much stronger than mine. Like me, the exalted Sultan is locked in that iron cage. He is waiting for the time when the prison bars will break and he can return to his homeland and suffuse the surroundings of this city with his fragrance.

When the Janab-i-Aalia heard the parrot's speech, her heart fluttered in its cage like a bird. And her imagination took flight. She decided that she would set out on a journey. That wise bird, that magical storyteller, screeched again: Allah Almighty is Truth, Allah is right. Right is His Prophet. Don't be oblivious of Him. Don't forget Him. Lo, Mallika-i-Aalia, this bird dares to submit that there is only one possibility on this journey. Travails and tribulations will be your fate as you travel from city to city. Huzoor will be condemned to wander from lane to lane, traverse interminable roads, and negotiate wild deserts. Upon reaching the destination, the consequences are already known. The British soldiers, armed with guns, guard the garden round the clock. Let alone a human being, even a bird does not dare to breach their security.

When the servants of the palace heard what the parrot said, they began to wail: First, the exalted Sultan, the pride of the Sultanat, left us, and now the glorious Mallika, the honour of the Sultanat, is preparing to leave. There will be riots in the city. Darkness will descend.

Soon, the news spread in every lane and square that the splendour of the city, the glorious Mallika, was going to leave that very day. The city was going to be left desolate. Hundreds of men and women, old and young came out of their houses, beating their breasts and wailing, determined to follow the Mallika and live in exile. The brave saddled their horses, tied turbans on their heads, draped shawls around their shoulders, gathered their arms, and set out to sacrifice their lives.

In that commotion, I recalled my revered father's instructions about taking a bird as a companion on the journey. I presented myself before the majestic Mallika and pleaded with her: O, Mallika of the world! This journey is perilous and the destination is far. The enemy is waiting for a chance. There are female spies watching each lane and square, relaying news of every movement of your blessed soul. Men in disguise surround you. There are treacherous men among our soldiers who keep the enemy posted about every move we make. Caution is necessary on this journey. Allow your servant to precede you with this parrot as my guide. We will keep a watch over the dangers and the perils along the way and keep you informed.

The Mallika-i-Aalia appreciated my proposal, called for a pen, wrote a letter addressed to the exalted Sultan, placed it in a cotton handkerchief, and tied it with a string of pearls took a ring off her little finger as a sign and handed it to me, her servant. After taking leave of the Mallika-i-Aalia, I went to inform Shahzad Mahal. But I was tongue-tied as soon as I saw her. I tried to muster courage, but failed. When she saw me in this dilemma, she urged me to speak. Then timidly, I disclosed to her my intention to undertake that journey. Though, she did not utter a word, her face turned pale. She sat like a statue for a long time. I too did not have the courage to speak. Then, agitated, she suddenly got up.

Worried and anxious, she walked back and forth between her room and the courtyard, mumbling to herself: Ya Ilahi, have mercy. My left eye has been twitching since the morning. A maid interjected: Bibi, you should not speak of evil omens at the time of parting. She was embarrassed by the chiding. She vowed that when I got back safely, she would cook a haziri meal and make an offering of a green alam at the dargah of Chhote Hazrat. Then she wrapped a silver coin in a piece of cotton and fastened it around my arm, saying: I place you in the custody of Imam-e-Zaamin. Show me your face when you return, as you are showing me your back at your departure. Her voice was tearful. Anxious, I looked at her and she began to cry. I could not hold myself any longer and instinctively moved forward to embrace her. This spelled calamity. She reclined her head on my shoulders and began to weep inconsolably. Warm tears streamed down her cheeks. Moved by her love, I kissed her wet cheeks. At the time of farewell, that faithful soul held the reins of my horse. I ran my fingers through her hair, which flowed gracefully down to her shoulders. Her fragrance lingered in my mind as I spurred my horse forward and set out on my journey.

As I rode past my family graveyard, I realised I was leaving the city of my ancestors. Who knows if I would ever return! I remembered all those ancestors who had died long ago, but whose graves had been freshly painted and marble headstones recently polished. And then I thought of all those unfortunate ones who had been massacred recently in some unknown lane, in some distant forest. They were not blessed enough either to find comfort in a grave or be wrapped in a shroud. My eyes welled up at that thought. I suddenly noticed a gazelle wandering restlessly amid the graves. I felt as though it was trying to stop me. I turned my gaze away and urged my horse swiftly forward. Soon, I left the city far, far behind. A blue jay, sitting on a tree on my left, flew right across my path. I shuddered for an instant, but the next moment I spurred my horse forward and we covered a vast distance in seconds.

I rode on for three days without a break—my body was glued to the saddle of the horse and my gaze was fixed on the parrot which flew above my head like a green shadow. On the third day of my journey, when night fell, I could not find a basti where I could rest. My horse was tired and slowing down, and I could no longer focus my gaze on the green shadow of the parrot above. Suddenly, I saw a comet streak across the sky. My heart sank and my mind was flooded with scores of doubts. Surrounded by hundreds of misgivings, I rode on with my gaze fixed on the comet. But, as I remembered the parrot and turned my gaze away from the comet to look for its green shadow, I was startled. The parrot had vanished. I had forgotten all my plans. I had lost my way.

Tote Mian paused. We thought he would resume his tale, but he kept gazing at the sky silently. The night had advanced and the surroundings were already drenched with dew. Soaked in the moonlight, the mango tree, providing shade to the parrot's grave, stood in silence. Raw mangoes were scattered around it, as though they had just fallen with the dewdrops. Tote Mian moved, stirred the heap of ash in front of him with a pair of tongs, picked up a smouldering ember, dropped it in his chillum, took long puffs, and began to gaze at the sky. We could not gather enough courage to ask him about what happened next. The night had already advanced and it was cold. We got up quietly and sadly returned to our homes.

Hakim Ji fell silent. He took the pipe of the huqqa from Adalat Ali, pressed its nozzle between his lips, closed his eyes, and began to puff. In the silence of the night, the gurgling sound of the huqqa echoed for a long time. Then he resumed: Tote Mian was a pious man. He took great care of others in their final moments, but when his own end came he did not bother anyone. None of us came to know about it. The moment he read the signs of his departure, he abandoned his routine, sent us away early in the night, and then lay down in his small room. Aladiya told us that he heard the parrots screeching in the morning. When they continued to screech incessantly and for a long time, he went to the orchard where Tote Mian lived, but Tote Mian was not there. Only the flock of parrots was screeching. Surprised, he wondered what could have happened to Tote Mian. He knocked at his door, but there was no response. When he opened the door, he saw that Tote Mian had passed away. There was peace on his face.

Adalat Ali silently puffed at his huqqa. Then he said: Hakim Ji, it's late now.

Hakim Ji answered: Oh, I was so engrossed in telling the tale that I didn't even realise the time. It's very late now. I have to wake up early.

Hakim Ji turned on his side and went to sleep. Adalat Ali's eyes too had begun to droop. Nasir was already snoring. But sleep eluded Ghani. He lay flat on his cot and gazed at the sky. The star-studded sky seemed as though countless nails from horseshoes were scattered across it; the sparks emanating from them were like the hoof-marks of all those gallant horses which had galloped down that path to the fields afar. In the East, he spotted a cluster of stars which resembled a horseshoe. As he gazed at it, he felt that he could hear the sound of galloping horses.

Glossary

Ai Bibi, Aji: Forms of address.

Alam: A 'flag' or 'sign' carried in battles. It is associated with Imam Husain's brother Abbas, the standard bearer (*Alamdar*) of Imam Husain's army.

Alha-Udal/Alha: Alha and Udal were children of Dasraj, a successful commander of the Chandel king Parmal. Alha is one of the heroes of the popular *Alha-Khand* ballad in Bundelkhand.

Amil: Necromancer, conjurer who recites spiritual incantation.

Anjanhari: Golden wasp.

Ashadh: The third month of the Hindu calendar marked by the monsoon. It corresponds with June-July of the Georgian calendar.

Ashrafi: Gold coin.

Azab-i-ilahi: Divine curse.

Azan: An Islamic call to prayer.

Azakhana: A house of mourning.

Baba Jan: Father.

Bada Bazaar: Central market of the town.

Bade Abba: Father's elder brother, tau in Hindi.

Bahannu: Sister-in-law.

Behna: Sister.

Bahu: Daughter-in-law.

Bakht Khan: (1797–1859) He was the commander-in-chief of Indian rebel forces in the struggle against the British in 1857.

Bela: Jasmina.

Bhadon: Fifth month of the Hindu calendar. It marks the beginning of autumn.

Bhai: Brother.

Bhuwand: Barren land.

Butarab: An epithet of Hazrat Ali, son-in-law of the Prophet; literally, father of the earth.

Chacha: Father's younger brother; uncle.

Chadar: Veil.

Chaliswan: The fortieth day ritual after the death of a person.

Chaat: A savoury snack, typically served at roadside stalls or food carts.

Chawk: Town square.

Chawki: A low wooden stool.

Chobedar: A mace-bearer or usher with silver mace.

Chilla: Literally means 'forty'. It refers to the spiritual practice of penance and solitude in Sufism. In this ritual, an ascetic attempts to sit in meditation without food for forty days in a solitary cell.

Chillum: A conical bowl with pipe used for smoking tobacco.

Cowrie: Seashell used as currency in ancient India and as late as nineteenth century in the eastern parts of India.

Dahi-bada: A popular snack prepared by soaking fried flour balls in thick yoghurt.

Dalhousie, Lord: Was the governor general of India between 1848–1856.

Dargah/Chhoti Dargah: Small tomb.

Dastarkhwan: Tablecloth or dining spread.

Deorhi: Entrance to a house; threshold; a veranda for ordinary visitors.

Faqir/Fakir: Derived from *faqr* meaning 'poverty'. A Dervish; also beggar.

Ganga, Jamuna, Saraswati: Names of three sacred Indian rivers.

Haider Ali: (1720–1782) Ruler of Mysore; fought the British in the first and the second Anglo-Mysore wars.

Hamzad: Persian for astral body. This divine creature is the self-image of a person. Though not visible to ordinary mortals, an amil can summon him with his special powers.

Haveli: A traditional townhouse or mansion.

Hazrat Raisul Ahrar: A title given to Maulana Muhammad Ali (1878–1931), the leader of the Khilafat Movement. Literally, a leader of the free people.

Haziri: Meal cooked for the *niyaz* of Hazrat Abbas, Imam Hussain's brother.

Hazrat Abbas: Abbās ibn 'Ali was the son of Imam Ali, the first Imam of Shia Muslims and Um-mul Banin. He was martyred in the battle of Karbala.

Huqqa: Hookah is a single or multi-stemmed instrument for smoking tobacco.

Ibn-Saud: Abdulaziz ibn Abdul Rahman ibn Faisal ibn Turki ibn Abdullah ibn Muhammad Al Saud was the founder of Saudi Arabia, who followed the puritanical Wahabi Islam. He demolished the graves and other symbols revered by Muslims, especially Shia Muslims.

Ikka: A horse carriage.

Ilahi: Godly.

Imambara: A shrine built by Shia Muslims for the purpose of mourning or Azadari.

Imam-i-mazloom: An epithet for Husain Ibn-Ali (Prophet Muhammad's grandson), slain in the battle of Karbala by the forces of Yazid.

Imam-i-Zamin: The eighth imam of Shias, Imam Ali ibne Musa ar-Reza, is also called Imam-e-Zaamin. Shia Muslims tie a coin in his name on their arms when they travel. The tradition probably came from the time when Mamun, an Abbasid caliph, put Imam Reza on the throne for strategic reasons and released coins in his name.

Isha: Evening prayer.

Insha Allah: God willing.

Jalali Wazifa: Literally means amount or a certain number. Here, it refers to a prayer recited to win God's favour and ward off the evil.

Jihad: A striving or a struggle with a praiseworthy aim.

Jyotishi: An astrologer.

Kansuri: A bird.

Khaddar/Khadi: Hand-spun cloth.

Khandal: A tree common in north India.

Khod: Helmet.

Khas: Fibrous roots. The Mughals devised *Khas ki tatti* for cooling their rooms.

Kothari: A small dark room, shed, cell.

Kothi: A mansion.

Khilafat: A pan-Islamic political protest campaign launched by Muslims of India to influence the British government not to abolish the Ottomon Caliphate.

Khood: Iron helmet worn by warriors.

Khyber: A mountain pass connecting the town of Landi Kotal, near the Afghanistan-Pakistan border, to the Valley of Peshawar.

Kunjdon wali Gali: The locality or lane of vegetable vendors.

Kachha: Unpaved.

Lahaul: *Lā ḥawla wa lā quwwata illā billāh*, which is usually translated as 'There is no might or power except Allah'. Recited by a Muslim to ward off difficulties.

Lal Mandir: Temple made of red bricks.

Madar: Sufi saint Syed Badiuddin Zinda Shah Madar (d. 1437 CE) whose shrine is in Makanpur, Kanpur. His followers are called Madariyya. The month of his Urs is called Madar. There are many madars in small towns.

Marsiya: An elegiac poem written to commemorate the martyrdom and valour of Hussain ibn Ali and his companions.

Masha Allah: An Arabic phrase that means 'God has willed' expresses appreciation, joy, praise, or thankfulness.

Majlis: Literally, 'a place of sitting'. Among the Shias, 'Majlis' refers to the gathering of people who remember and mourn Ahl-al-Bayt and Imam Hussain's martyrdom.

Maula Mushkil Kusha: Mushkil Kusha is one who can ease difficulty. It is the title of Imam Ali ibn-Abu Talib, the son-in-law of the Prophet.

Mir Anis (1803–1874): A major Urdu poet. The lines quoted roughly mean: 'The fiery sun of Imamat has set out on its journey even in adversity, and the silvery moon still revolves around it.'

Mohalla: A country subdivision or neighbourhood.

Muharram: The first month of Islamic calendar. Shia Muslims, observe it as the month of martyrdom of Hussein ibn Ali.

Munajat: A sacred song in praise of God or holy souls sung to ask for favours or deliverance from calamities.

Muhammad Ali (1878–1931): Maulana Mohammad Ali Jauhar was an Indian Muslim leader, activist, journalist, scholar, and a poet, and was among the leading figures of the Khilafat Movement.

Munshiji: A secretary or a language teacher.

Naad-i-Ali: A prayer which is a call to Ali to help resolve difficulties.

Nauroz: Persian New Year. It marks the beginning of spring. It occurs on 21 March.

Paandan: A small box used to store betel leaves and some condiments.

Pankha: Fan made of cloth or bamboo. The hanging pankha is a heavy cloth fixed to the ceiling and pulled by a rope to stir the air.

Patka: The sash that adorns the alam.

Pankha/Punkha: A fan made of bamboo sticks.

Pirji: Title for spiritual master or Sufi guide.

Rahat: Persian wheel.

Raam Naam: Lord Ram.

Roti: Indian bread.

Qasai Mohalla: A neighbourhood inhabited by butchers.

Salar-i-Azam: Lieutenant general.

Sarauta: Nutcracker.

Sarkar: Person of position of authority.

Sawan: Fourth month of Hindu calendar or July-August of Georgian calendar. Along with Ashadh, it occurs in monsoon season.

Shaukat Ali: Maulana Shaukat Ali (10 March 1873–26 November 1938) was an Indian Muslim nationalist and a leader of the Khilafat Movement.

Sher Shah: Sher Shah Suri (1486–1545) defeated the Mughal emperor Humayun in 1540. He is known for his administrative reforms and for building the Grand Trunk Road.

Sijdegaah: A place where a worshipper prostrates herself/himself. Shias use a clay piece from the battlefield of Karbala as a place of prostration during their prayers.

Siparah: There are thirty Siparahs or Juz in the Quran.

Sultanat: A state or a country governed by a Sultan.

Surahi: Clay pitcher used for storing drinking water.

Surkhab: A bird, species of lark.

Taal: A lumberyard.

Taya: Uncle; father's elder brother.

Tahmat: A loin cloth.

Tai Amma: Wife of Father's elder brother, Tai in Hindi.

Tatiya Tope: Nickname of Ramachandra Pandurang Tope (1814–18 April 1859), notable general in the first battle of freedom against the British in 1857.

Tauba: To vow to sin no more; to repent (of evil, sin, crime, and so on); to recant.

Tazia/Taziya: A colourfully painted bamboo and paper mausoleum taken out by Shia Muslims as a part of ritual procession on 'Ashura', the tenth day of Muharram.

Teeja: Rituals observed on the third day after death.

Thanedar: Police station in-charge.

Thatheri Wali Gali: The locality or lane of brass smiths.

Tilism-i-Hoshruba: The mid-nineteenth-century Urdu epic fantasy by Muhammad Husain Jah (d. 1899).

Tipu Sultan: Tipu Sultan (1750–1799), also known as the 'Tiger of Mysore', ruled Mysore. He was defeated by the British in the Fourth Anglo-Mysore War on 4th May 1799.

Topi: Cap or hat.

Tulsi: Basil.

Upala: Dried cow-dung cake used for fuel.

Wuzu: Ablution before offering Namaz.

Ya Ilahi: O God!

Zari: An ornate, usually a gilded, lattice structure that encloses a grave in a mosque or Islamic shrine and serves as a symbol of their sacred nature.

Zenana: The part of a house for the seclusion of women.

Zohr: Noon-time prayer.